AND THE GODS OF LOVE RETIRED

AND THE GODS OF LOVE RETIRED

KRISHNA V R MUPPAVARAPU

PARTRIDGE
A Penguin Random House Company

Cover design: Ankur Bhushan http://ankurbhushan.com

ISBN:	Softcover	978-1-4828-1540-5
	Ebook	978-1-4828-1539-9

To order additional copies of this book, contact
Partridge India
000 800 10062 62
www.partridgepublishing.com/india
orders.india@partridgepublishing.com

CONTENTS

To all the dreamers in this beautiful world

Disclaimer

It is not the author's intention to endorse drinking and smoking when he refers to them in some of his stories. Also, any reference to specific professions or religious beliefs is not intentional. Any treatment by the author that has a controversy-generating potential is to be seen purely as a means of artistic expression. What matters at the end of it all is if the world has enough love in it.

ACKNOWLEDGMENTS

It is the most difficult to acknowledge the contributions that go into creating a piece of art. Different works draw inspirations from different sources. But an inspiration common to this work and to my earlier work is my loving wife Sirisha. She will remain one in all my future works and forever.

The unadulterated and unconditional love of our two sons Ishaan and Arkaan gives me ample space to think of all beautiful things in life. This book is definitely a manifestation of the love for life the little rascals instilled in me. It would not be too far in time when they grow up to understand what this book means.

Then I have a whole set of wonderful friends, colleagues, seniors and family who are with me, encouraging and urging me to keep writing. That encouragement simply is priceless.

The credit for the stunning cover page goes to Ankur Bhushan—my friend and a professional portrait and still-life photographer. Her inputs also helped in organizing the contents of the book.

The beautiful dreamy interiors became possible only because of Prasad and Sai who creatively captured the stories in a series of complex illustrations.

And then there is YOU, the reader who just encouraged me by laying your hands and sights on my creation. I am hopeful that you will like this work and bless me with the conviction that I can keep writing with passion and without being unduly worried about the returns on my efforts.

Last but not the least I express my sincere gratitude to the gods and goddesses of love who agreed to write a beautiful foreword that sets the tone for your journey into a world of fantasies, love and happiness.

FOREWORD

We narrated these stories to the author in his dreams. When he invited us into his dreams we were surprised to see that he was consumed by single-mindedness about writing a beautiful book on love and romance—a subject that had been our forte traditionally.

In fact we got the ideas for all these stories from the experiences we had as we travelled the length and breadth of the universe trying to find out the most love-laden planet. While we did have an idea that we could expect a lot from the earth, little did we know that our experiences with the humankind would force us into retirement. The earth is so full of love that we started feeling redundant on such a beautiful planet.

Having narrated the stories of love to the author, we waited for a while loitering around on the earth to see how the stories would look like when frame-worked in a book. When we saw the first copy of the book, we realized that the author had done more than what we expected and he must be complimented for creating such a masterpiece. We feel proud that he has done real justice to our stories.

"Divine Game of Chance" is a heartrending account of a couple's tryst with destiny and how they overcame the grief. The collection of dreams "Gods of Love Want to Dream" is really a bold attempt at exploring the mechanics of dreams. And then of course the short stories that are so unique are something that cannot be missed even for the best things in life.

Now we have collectively decided to take retirement from our job of creating love in the universe. Instead we will go back and spend our time spreading the message of the earthly love in other worlds, but not before congratulating the author on coming up with a superb collection of OUR stories.

We are sure this book makes a wonderful gift to your loved ones.

~ *The Gods and Goddesses of Love (now retired)*

Scribble your love notes

The Heavenly Secrets

They both reached heaven within a year of each other. She departed first, and unable to bear the separation, he decided to follow her. It was not as if they were too old to have died, but they were not very young too.

She was brought up in a house of devout believers whereas he, in a house that believed in an external force but did not care much for it. When alive, neither of them had any preconceived notions about how heaven looked like.

As he climbed the stairs to heaven he expected her to receive him, but was disappointed that she was not there. He wondered about what could have happened to her. He was sure that for all her virtuousness his wife would have come to heaven.

He entered heaven and was impressed by the setup. The environment was pleasant and everyone around seemed very happy in general. He could see in their faces a great sense of contentedness. But there were a few of them who looked a bit tensed and flustered. A few others were being forced out of heaven by bouncer-angels. He asked one of the passing-by officers of heaven about the tense looking inmates only to be told that they were under a kind of probation. They had been unfaithful to their partners while on earth and presumably that was the only sin they committed. Those sinners had to pass a battery of tests to absolve themselves of the earthly sin to take up a permanent residence in heaven. The officer also told him that the souls being shunted out of heaven had failed the test and quite logically their final destination was hell.

He had jitters hearing what the officer had to tell him, knowing very well that he was also to be placed on probation. He was hoping against hope that by some freak technical error in the records of heaven his name should not figure in the probationary residents list. But his fears came true when his name appeared on top of the list of the unfaithful. He was literally a worried soul. He tried in vain to know in advance the kind of test he had to pass. All he was told was that the test would be a nominal one and passing would not be that difficult a task. He was kept waiting for days together for his turn to take the tests. Each day of waiting multiplied his anxiety and agony to the extent that one day he almost broke down.

At the same time a sense of remorse started consuming him and he was feeling terribly sorry for his wife. He thought that he should not have lent himself to those tempting situations when he had an understanding wife who was always loyal to him.

As he was being heralded to the test area he started thinking about the good time he had with his wife and was hoping to catch up with her very soon. But somewhere he feared if she indeed were dispatched to hell.

His turn for taking the test came after a long agonizing wait and he was let into a narrow lane. He was told that he had to cross the lane to go to his next test. As he entered the lane he saw embers of fire strewn on the floor. He was told that he had to walk over the fire and would be deemed to have passed the test only if nothing happened to his feet or body. The very sight of the red embers gave him reasons enough to believe that what he committed while on earth was not a minor sin, nor was this test as nominal as it was portrayed initially. He stood there for a while not knowing what to do. The mental pressure he was experiencing was unbearable. At a point he almost gave up and was about to tell the officers that he was fine to go to hell rather than walking over fire. But he reconciled to the fact that hell would be worse than the fire and realized that he did not have an option but to try his luck walking over the embers.

He closed his eyes in an act of seeking forgiveness from his wife and earnestly meditated on a prospect that given a chance to live again he would do so only with her and never be unfaithful to her again. Eyes still closed, he started walking in the lane. When he opened his eyes he was surprised to see that the lane with the fire was behind him and he came out unhurt. He realized that it was his remorse towards his beloved wife that saved him from failing the test and being thrown into hell.

He then went from one test to another coming out of all of them successfully. The sharp objects on the floor could not puncture his feet, the huge rotating blades did not cut him and the venomous snakes did not bite him. His love for his wife compounded and he was now longing to meet her. He took a vow of faithfulness and loyalty.

He entered the last component of the battery of tests in which he was pushed into a room and the doors got locked by themselves from outside. Inside the room lay a beautiful figure on a huge bed that was as white as the full moon. She was naked but for a brief that barely covered her modesty. She was endowed with assets that even the goddesses of love would feel jealous about. Her moist lips looked so inviting that even the masters of celibacy could probably not resist. In essence she was romance personified. More interestingly she had her hands tied to the cot with a velvety cloth making her look even more inviting.

For a moment he was awe-struck. The next moment he found himself almost on the verge of occupying her. His mind was numb and his physical senses started taking control of him. Carnal instincts started working overtime. He knew subconsciously that this was a test he had to pass to become a permanent resident of heaven. He knew the moment he touched her he would be chucked into hell. But he was feeling overwhelmed by the strength of the instincts that were haunting him even after death. He was in a state of helpless recklessness driven by a strong desire.

Then as if in a twist of providence he remembered his wife and the resolutions of loyalty he made as he passed through the earlier tests. The moment the realization crossed his mind, he could sense a retraction of the humanly instincts. He could now feel the real heaven. The beauty in front of him no longer commanded his senses—he was in total control.

A whisperer-angel hovered around his ear humming a song that indicated his successful passing of all the tests. The doors of the room opened automatically and an officer handed over heavenly robes to him, announced him a permanent resident of heaven and vanished from there. To his surprise divine clothes now adorned the beauty that appeared just a few celestial moments ago, as naked as a newborn. The velvet cloth that tied her hands now was no longer there. She rose from the bed, stood in front of him with arms folded and told him her own secrets. She told him how she had been waiting for ages in that room for a soul to come that would not touch her. She thanked him profusely for releasing her from the curse for having been unfaithful to her husband. And then she walked away into her new home—the heaven.

He wished he were subjected to all those tests whenever he felt like being disloyal to his wife while he was still alive. He wished he died every time he wanted to be unfaithful.

As he walked into heaven with a sense of relief and also feeling sorry for his beloved wife, the whiff of a familiar perfume hit his face. Through the dreamy mist of the garden he could see his wife walking towards him. He was blown away by the ecstasy of seeing his beloved again. She looked as gorgeous and as desirable as she was during her prime. They came together and held each other in a tight embrace.

After a while, he sat her down on a bench and knelt before her. He wanted to say, "Honey, I am happy that we are back together. But I must confess that I had to pass through an ordeal to reach you. I beg your forgiveness for having been unfaithful to you . . ." She too wanted to tell him the secret that she had to wait in the testing room for the right soul to come and relieve her. She wanted to tell him how awkward she felt each time a stranger touched her and how exploited she felt for days and nights together. Neither of them spoke what they wanted to, because they both knew it did not matter any longer.

They "lived" happily ever after.

The Romantic Chessboard

He found it difficult to digest that his favorite heroine showed some of her most unexpected angles in the newly released film. He had been following all of her movies without fail, but this was the first film in which the actress shed her regular image of the girl-next-door to play the role of a seductress.

He always had a great adoration for her that actually bordered on possessiveness. "How could she possibly smoke?" he thought riding back home, "Did she really have to take her top off?" The smoking act, coupled with her erotic presentation added to his sensual woes.

In bed, unable to sleep, he kept on thinking about the various aspects of the movie that showed his screen goddess in a light that he never expected nor was exposed to till then.

He did not realize when he fell asleep. He in fact had started playing chess just recently and the intensity of the game was so much that he often experienced dreams that had huge chess pieces moving from one square to the other of a great chess board. But that night he had one of the most disturbing dreams in which he got passionately involved in a game of chess with his favorite actress. He dreamed of the lady standing in the queen's position of a chequered board, wearing an appealing red gown. He saw himself as a pawn moving at the instructions of his queen. He dreamed of carrying out forbidden activities that the queen ordered him to do. She was too hot for him to handle and had an aura of sexy arrogance around her. He was overwhelmed by the unorthodox overtures thrown by the fantastic dream, not to say that he knew what orthodox stuff meant at all—he was still a fifteen year old boy who had no realistic exposure to matters of instinct. It was still a fantasy for him.

A dream being a dream, he woke up to the morning alarm in his clock just at a time when his mistress was about to reveal herself in entirety. He shook his head as a gesture of disbelief. He was disappointed that the dream ended short of an exciting climax.

What followed were days of dreaming and nights of sleeplessness. He was constantly thinking of what he could have seen had the alarm not gone off. Nights were difficult to bear. He was lost in a state of confusion not knowing how to deal with the situation. His mind was not his; disturbing and provocative thoughts about his demi-goddess occupied his otherwise intelligent brain.

The queen of his dreams was growing from strength to strength and he was cherishing his dream-slavery to her. He started spending a lot of time trying creative outlets for the intense emotions he was passing through, but no amount of venting could help ease the sweet burden created by the pleasure centers of his brain.

Everyone including his teachers was flabbergasted by a sudden change in his demeanor and an uncharacteristic dip in his grades. From being a consistent first ranker in the class he now was ranking only second or third. Constant inquiries from his parents or teachers did not reveal the reasons for the aberration. His parents were concerned but could not do much about bringing him back to his normal self. His participation in extra-curricular activities came to a literal naught and his friends missed his brilliance.

Then one day a realization dawned upon him that obsession with his dream girl was not going to take him anywhere and was in fact interfering with the goals he had set for himself in life. He put his highly evolved brain to work and started working aggressively to ward off the influence of the matinee idol. What ensued were some of the most unsettling resolutions by him that could have a material impact on his future.

As a first step he picked up a popular book on self-restraint and started following the prescriptions to the tee. Grueling sessions of meditation and ironically tough mind-relaxation techniques became a significant part of his day. However uncomfortable they were, cold water baths before sleeping and early in the morning seemed to be able to temper his senses. He stopped playing chess and instead started physical workouts as a means of diverting his attention from the heroine. Movies were now a forbidden thing for him, as were the hot magazines that he always had in his room. He vowed not to allow even a single thought of the opposite sex distract him. This routine of abstinence and self-denial continued for the next many years during which he excelled in everything from studies to extracurricular activities. But matters of the procreation instinct were buried away in the abyss of his self-imposed discipline.

He passed his school and college with distinction and went on to become a great scholar. He was now a much sought after consultant with many big firms and was earning handsomely—his long cherished dream. With a superb physique that he built over years of strenuous workouts earned him a lot of admirers—mostly girls and young women. But constant apathy to anything female made him oblivious of the following he had both at work and outside.

His friends wondered why he shied away from topics related to women, love, sex and marriage. There were a few who thought he had problems with his manhood. But his physical appearance never allowed even the doubters to consolidate their opinion about him.

But what he did not know was that he had a secret follower in his workmate—a gorgeous lady in her late twenties, probably just a bit older than him. He shared an excellent working relationship with her. The two as a team were considered top notch when it came to delivering business results. They competed with each other, they collaborated, they quarreled and they reconciled. But the business outcome was nothing short of brilliant fireworks. What he did not know was that she always fantasized about being with him. She had her mind full with thoughts about him and dreamed of having babies with him. She always wondered about her own inability to express what she thought about him—probably something to do with the cultural upbringing that was characteristic of the society in which she grew up. In fact she could never talk to him about anything personal. He would always spurn her attempts to raise anything that had to do with their personal lives.

She tried many things to grab his attention but all her efforts were futile—he spoke only business and nothing else. One day, they were working late hours and the assignment extended late into the night. On that particular day, he noticed something about her that he did not till then. Something about her had changed—he was trying to figure that out but was unable to. At the end of a marathon work session on the difficult assignment, they decided to call it a day.

He reached home and slipped into his night dress. Thoroughly exhausted, he lay down in his bed even without bothering to eat. Sleep came almost immediately, and so did a dream. He saw a dream that disturbed him after many years. In the dream he saw a huge chess board. In the queen's position was the most beautiful woman in a tantalizing red dress and he was in a pawn's position taking orders from her. He executed all the orders and that included extending a sort of physical gratification to the queen on her demand. She was all over him provoking him at the wrong places for the right reasons. Interestingly she had a bell in her one hand and was ringing it. The more she touched him, the louder the bell rang. As she went down on her knees he could see her ringing the bell more profusely. Just coinciding with the initiation of the ultimate act of aggression by her, the ringing of the bell in her hand transformed into the ringing of the morning alarm in his watch. He woke up to a jolt that was also the result of a sudden vent of his pent-up instincts.

He rose from his bed and started to get ready for work. He gave a strange look at his night pants before throwing them away into the wash-bin, bathed and dressed up. Within no time he was in his car. But he could not stop thinking about the dream he saw the previous night. He was wondering about what could have happened had the clock alarm not gone off. He had a doubt that the girl in his dream was none other than his workmate. But she reminded him of someone else too.

At work he was finding it difficult to focus on the assignment and was literally fixated on his beautiful friend. She too was giving him knowing glances making him wonder what she really meant. He started realizing that she had made certain changes to her make-up. Her hairstyle looked a bit different, reminiscent of a style that was in vogue years ago. The mascara gave her eyes a sensual appeal. Her red lipstick made her lips look tempting as if the lips represented an insider view of her inner secrets. He could not figure out if the blush on her cheeks was a natural one or if it was made up. But more intriguingly her red dress was strikingly similar to the one the dream girl wore the previous night. He had his eyes fixated on her endowments.

The day passed by and he found himself consumed by fantasies about her. He did notice her smile and giggle a lot. The day end came and when she asked him to be dropped at her home in his car, he agreed without the slightest hesitation.

It was already dark when they reached her home. She courteously invited him into the house and made him sit down as she went into the kitchen to make some coffee for both of them. As she walked towards him with the cups in her hands, he could not resist the view offered by her near-perfect figure that reminded him of his favorite heroine of yesteryear. She handed over a cup to him and offered him to show the house. He was being taken around the house sipping into his coffee as much as he was sipping on her beauty.

As they entered the bedroom he was impressed by the colors and shades of the room. They were just romantic. He was appreciating her aesthetic sense. But at the same time he could sense that a certain instinct that he forbade all these years was waking up within him. Just about when he thought he should take control of his instinct, he looked down only to see that the bedroom had chequered tiles of black and white that looked like the squares of a huge chess board. When he lifted his eyes from the floor, he found her standing seductively in the queen's position. He was feeling like a pawn ready to take his queen's orders.

This time the alarm in his watch did not go off. A vow of abstinence was broken even as vows of a new life were being exchanged. She had a smile of vicarious satisfaction writ on her face.

A Barber Cannot Cut His Own Hair

Romance was in the air. Couples thronged the place that was tactically located on the outskirts of the city. The setting was suggestive. The subtle blueness emanating from the neon lamps complemented the pink color of the walls. Spirits flowed freely and it appeared as if new and exotic cocktails were getting discovered by the minute. There were sippers and then there were guzzlers. Swapping was rampant and no one seemed to be bothered about the complexities that it could create for them in their futures.

She found herself cozying up to a handsome young man who she never met before nor was sure of meeting again. Nevertheless she could not resist side-glancing her boyfriend who was getting busy with another stunning beauty. She could sense a similar curiosity in her boyfriend's eyes but the alcohol had already numbed her senses. She was only marginally aware of

XXX

her surroundings. Through the loud music she tried to decipher what her new partner was saying and blabbered back something.

The music got louder and the acts became bolder. The haziness created by the smoke did its part in stoking up the passions. Gradually the scenario grew wilder and whatever sense of logic that prevailed till then evaporated into thin air and amalgamated with the smoke. The visual was like a wild fantasy that could exist only in dreams.

It took not more than a few minutes for her to come back into reality and realize that the raunchy visual that was playing was just a video he brought home that day. She was thoroughly enjoying the show. For a moment she felt happy for the fact that he had started showing interest in matters of love after a long time. There was a phase in their married life when he had turned completely impassive in spite of her best efforts to present herself in the most desirable format. She was delighted to see him change. The video played on and on as they started rediscovering their passions.

Days passed by and she could see him transform into his earlier self who used to keep her sleepless for nights together. While she was happy to see him change, a germ of suspicion got implanted in her sensitive heart. She wondered how a person who was inert for almost three years could change all of a sudden. As she kept thinking about it, the suspicion grew bigger and created a labyrinth of thoughts that overshadowed the happiness she felt. Her primary suspicion was that of his involvement outside the wedlock.

Though she guarded her personal secrets ferociously, she gave in to the temptation of consulting her best friends during their noon meetings. Each of them had a story to tell her that made her feel even more insecure. Most of the stories pointed to an external source of inspiration for his changed attitude.

She unleashed her feminine instincts and it became a regular affair for her to secretly scrutinize every act of her husband. She smelt his shirt every evening only to feel the strong odor of the special cigars he smoked—a habit which she always persuaded him to quit. She compulsively checked the pockets of his shirts and trousers. She checked his wallet to see if he was stocking any emergency items that could prove his indulgence outside. She sneaked into his computer after he slept and searched his emails—both personal and official. She checked his bank account to see any abnormal money transactions. She smelled the interiors of his car and cast a magnified vision to locate any strands of hair that were not his. When at home she found herself constantly looking into the mirror but she had a bias that made her believe firmly that she did not grow any more desirable than what she was earlier.

Days of inquiry and scrutiny did not yield any conclusive answers. She was perplexed with herself. A thought that her suspicion could be baseless created a sense of guilt in her otherwise strong conscience. Every night of love making made her more frigid. She only hoped that he did not realize her faked feelings in bed lest his respect for her should go down had he had no vice on his side.

As days passed by without any breakthrough in her investigation, she harbored nearly self-destructive thoughts ranging from hiring a private detective to filing for divorce. Her best friends added fuel to fire by indoctrinating her. But somewhere in a small corner of her sensible heart she trusted his loyalty to her.

Many days later one day she waved him goodbye as he left for work and came inside the house only to realize that he had forgotten to take his favorite bag along. She picked up her phone to call him and remind him. But as if ordained by instinct she put the phone down and instead opened the bag which she had not done for years. As she opened the bag she wondered how she missed as important a component as a bag in her investigative stint.

Inside the bag was his grooming kit that apparently he had not used for many years. She remembered that it was her first gift to him as they got engaged. There was a fading photograph of him and her that was taken when they were newly married. Then there was an early photograph of their two children who were now grown up enough to go off to foreign lands for their higher studies. There was a copy of the first certificate their son got for winning a running race when he was hardly five years of age. The first bangles their little daughter wore found a place in a cool corner of the bag. The bag looked like a lovely miniature universe with all artifacts pointing to something about the family. She wondered as to where he got the collection when as a homemaker she herself did not quite remember or knew of the existence of those beautiful relics. A sense of nostalgia gripped her and a tear dropped from her eye. She was feeling awful as she started realizing that her suspicion about him was unfounded. But the poison in her mind was so powerful that another tear that was about to drop from her eye literally rolled itself back.

She again started searching the bag frantically for possible evidences of his purported infidelity. And finally she stumbled upon a book that looked like an old diary. She never saw him write his diary and was getting curious to know what was inside. Quickly she flipped the pages only to realize that the dairy was very old and it had dates that preceded their marriage. Most of the pages were filled with some gibberish and a few poems and short stories he had written when he was young. He often used to boast to her about his poetic skills but she was never interested in his poems or his short stories.

Just about when she was closing the diary it occurred to her that the last few pages had something peculiar about them. The pre-printed dates were struck through and instead there were very recent dates written by hand. Anxiously she started reading the pages, wondering what prompted him to start writing the diary again after so many years. Each page had a revelation for her. The first thing he wrote was about his visit to the psychiatrist because of newly developed symptoms of depression and the psychiatrist's advice to maintain a diary of his thoughts. As she read through, she was amazed by the fact that he had only one thing to write about—his love for her. In many pages he wrote about his inability to take care of her as much as he wished to and how much that bothered him. As she read through she was touched by his concern and caring for her. The labyrinth of suspicious thoughts that held her mind hostage was giving way to clear channels of faith and love. She realized that her guilt of misunderstanding him was coming true and that bore heavily on her conscience. The adamant tear in her eye that rolled itself back a few moments ago now brought along with it many more tears that were landing without noise in her lap.

Through the sense of relief and remorse, she managed to finish the most recent post in the diary, when she started rolling with laughter. The last few posts were a bunch of hilariously incoherent thoughts. The pages read, "Today confessed to my close friend about inability to perform in bed. Did it after a lot of hesitation . . . Friend gave me a video to take home and watch along with 'wifey'. Came home early from work and watched the video alone when wife was away shopping. Felt good about it. Haven't seen a video for years . . . Didn't have the time . . . Watched it again with sweetheart in the night . . . Could see she was happily enjoying it. First day of success in bed after three years [*sic*].

"Today was a good day; a big day for me. Found myself. Thought sweetheart loved me in bed after long time. I too found her very hot. Think office work was too much for me that I stopped noticing her sexiness. Video helped me find the time for my darling [*sic*].

"Today was the best day . . . Could see new angles of sweetheart . . . Didn't know she knew so many techniques . . . Whoa! Nothing but time . . . Realized that spending time with her is the trick. I love woman on top. Darling takes the lead, I am happy. Delegating responsibility and authority is good—not only at work but also in bed [*sic*].

"Today went to the psychiatrist's office and told him about the good things happening in life . . . Told him watching video helped me . . . He felt offended . . . But told him that his treatment also helped . . . and convinced him not to feel bad . . . He told me his personal stuff and is now asking me for the video . . . I know a barber cannot cut his own hair and I don't need psychiatrist anymore [*sic*]"

As she read her husband's writings, through uncontrollable laughter she marveled the dichotomy that was him—the same person who scribbled childishly in his diary ran one of the most successful businesses in the city. She could understand his constraints in not letting her know about his weaknesses; but she felt he could rather have communicated to her.

That night she could literally feel her frigidity thaw in the warmth of the naked embrace. Playing with her tongue seductively she murmured into his ear, "You need to work on your communication, stupid!" He gave her an amused look and through the heavy breath replied, "I am a great communicator. People in my office respect me for my communication skills. What makes you think that I do not communicate? But why are you telling me at this time?" Even before he spoke any further her slender legs wound around his bare back and her lips locked his, as if in an attempt to hide from him the fact that she rediscovered herself through his rambling diary.

Her bouts of giggles through the night kept him guessing even as they both wandered in a fantasy world of unending possibilities. The subtle blueness emanating from the bed lamp complemented the pink color of the walls and any sense of logic that prevailed till then evaporated into thin air.

Story Of The Two Clocks

She grabbed his shoulder firmly and buried her face into his broad chest. She snuggled up to him as if to seek reassurance that he was not leaving her. Of late she had been suffering from pangs of depression. Medical checkups showed nothing abnormal—it was probably just a hormonal disharmony triggered by constant hard work and a complete negligence of her health. But her state of mind was so bad that it threw her life out of balance. Her clock had only two intervals—one was a twenty-hour interval occupied by the kids and the other was a four-hour interval in which she kept thinking and planning her twenty-hour interval.

She remembered the initial days of her marriage when she used to take the lead in the countless naughty encounters. He acknowledged many times that it was she who made him realize the passion of manhood. Many of the encounters were nonstop sessions of

24
3
6
9
12
15
18
21

lovemaking. But now she was so exhausted both physically and mentally that she no longer had that drive in her to keep up with his tempo. She knew very well that he was not a person who would go seeking pleasure outside the confines of the sweet little home they had built for themselves. She knew how he calmed himself because he always did it only with her approval. But the thoughts of a vibrant past coupled with those of a relatively lackluster present weighed heavily on her depressed soul. A fear started creeping into her mind that the lack of intimacy could alienate him from her.

As she cozied up to him he tried convincing her against the unfounded thoughts of separation. But the assurances had only a temporary effect on her. He did not know how to deal with the situation nor could he convince her about his faithfulness to her.

He started reading a lot about female psychology and aspects like depression and frigidity. He spent money going to counselors of all sorts. He would go to a counselor alone for he did not want to make his wife too conscious about her problems—he knew that taking her along would only compound and complicate the problem at hand.

As he researched more and more about it, he started getting strange and unexpected perspectives of the situation. As he dug deeper he realized that the problem was not with her but with his own self. He was surprised to know that he was solely responsible for the situation she was in. He quickly set out to make amends.

One of the first things he did was to announce his commitment to taking care of the kids for at least an hour or two every day. He started enjoying the way kids looked forward to listening to stories he had to tell at bedtime. Weekend coffee-making was his duty now and she was amazed to drink coffee that tasted so different. He occasionally cooked lunch and dinner for the family. For her the taste was so different that she wondered naively how poor a cook she had been all the while. Friday evenings were invariably meant for outings to new places—sometimes with the kids in tow and sometimes with the kids left to the care of their grandparents who lived in a different part of the same city. He created a complete change in the way the home functioned. There was more harmony at home now and kids acted less cranky than before.

All this came as a great refreshing change to her. Her clock now looked better with a new interval getting added—an interval meant only for him and her together. Nights and days did not hold any difference for them as far as intimacy was concerned. He was surprised to learn that his sweetheart had so many untapped talents with her. In bed she taught him new lessons of intimacy reminding him of the drive she had in the early days of marriage.

Days and nights passed. She had a mature glow in her face that came to her through a sense of great fulfillment and accomplishment. She thanked him as often as she could by simply offering herself to him physically, mentally and emotionally. She was sure that he would not leave her and that too forever.

Years later on a wintry weekend morning the two sat in the verandah watching the now grown up kids play with other kids from the neighboring houses. He made the weekend coffee as usual. Sipping through the coffee he grabbed her hand firmly and leaned onto her shoulder. He snuggled up to her as if to seek reassurance that she was not going to desert him.

She looked at his clock and realized that it had only two intervals. The twenty-hour interval was all for his office work as he grew professionally and got promoted to assume a higher responsibility at office. The remaining four-hour interval was for worrying about his twenty-hour interval. "Where does he find the time to spend with me and the kids?" she wondered taking a closer look at his clock. She shivered as she realized that his clock had more than twenty four hours. A further analysis revealed that he chronically borrowed the additional hours from the next day so as to balance his personal and professional lives—he was sleeping only a few hours a day. She now knew the reasons for his performance or the lack of it.

She knew she had her task cut out. The clock just turned around signifying a strange cycle called life.

The Book Of Wild Fantasies

The sea breeze caressed her flowing hair as if enamored by her beauty. The hot sun was busy tanning away her bare body, disappointed only slightly by the two pieces of cloth that adorned her secrets. Pearls of sweat were trying to find their way into her whirlpool-like navel. The beach sand was happily getting crushed under the warm weight of her curvaceous body that seemed like a perfect sculpture. The sky was all eyes for her beauty. The cosmic elements were lost in a funny competition.

Unmindful of the activity around her, she lay on the beach reading her favorite book on romance. The book was about a girl and a boy and the stories of their escapades in a world of wild fantasies. Each story she read from the book roused her in many ways. Feelings of amour engulfed her and she let loose the horses of her lusty imagination. As the imagination started to have a physical manifestation, she looked

around consciously if someone was noticing her. But she realized that she had no reason to worry—almost everyone around seemed to be in a similar state of mind and body; or at least she thought so.

With the book in one hand, her acts of exploration became rampant. She was getting an exhibitionistic thrill out of the solo escapade. The next moment she found herself under the voyeuristic gaze of a young man who lay in the same sands a few yards away from her. Though she enjoyed the attention she did feel a bit odd about it. With great difficulty she composed herself back into her normal state, but parts of her, including her mind were still throbbing from the sweet pain she inflicted upon herself.

She gazed back at the young man who seemed to have gotten through his teenage just a few years ago. Going by her judgment about the young man she knew he desired her—the lust in his eyes very evident. She instinctively knew by the proportions of his facial components that he had a strong masculine constitution. She let loose the horses of imagination once again—but this time it was only fantasies.

As the sun became more scorching, she got up, dressed herself in a tantalizing gown and started walking towards her hut-like lodging. She had a feeling that the young man was stalking her but did not bother to confirm. Without even looking back she just walked into her hut. The burden of instinct that started a while ago was now becoming difficult for her to manage. She had to do something about it and ended up continuing from where she left on the beach. She needed a companion and at that point in time he existed in her fantasies—the young man on the beach.

As the sun was setting she walked out of the hut half-drunk with her favorite spirit. She was scouting for newer means of recreation. While she was drinking inside her hut she did find the bearer attractive, but her priority was the young man on the beach. She staggered on the beach under the influence of the alcohol, her eyes intuitively searching for the young man.

She walked for miles along the beach enjoying the cool breeze that seemed to stoke up her passion and mood. She chose a reclusive spot and lay down on the beach watching the sun set over the edge of the vast body of water in front of her. The high tide kept reminding her of the turbulence she was passing through and familiar feelings doused her mind. She lay there for hours fantasizing. She fantasized about being the girl in her favorite book. She was in love with her loneliness and with herself. She was in love with the young man. She was in love with the full moon and the bright stars. Everything seemed perfectly set for a romantic rendezvous with the man of her fantasies—the star-lit sky, the full moon, the romance-laden breeze, the tickling murmurs of the tide and the man who existed in her fantasies. She dreamed of traveling to forbidden places indulging in pleasantly illogical acts along with her fantasy man.

As the cool breeze started turning cold, she walked back drudgingly to her hut. Digging into a special dish the bearer served, she looked around for her book only to realize that it was not there. She then remembered she had left it on the beach in the morning and was sure that she lost it forever. She was disappointed—she had the book handy especially when she loved herself. But that night she did not feel the loss too much. She had the company of her fantasy man and her drink. The more she drank the more help she got from him. It was a wild night.

The next day morning she woke up to the knock on her door. Drunk from the fantasies and oblivious of her own physical condition she opened the door to see the bearer waiting with a kettle in his hand. She ordered him in. She was still in the dreamy world of fantasies that blew her away through the night. She could sense the bearer's uneasiness about her dress strewn across the room in a way that was suggestive of the wildness that existed the previous night. She could also sense the bearer's glances through her revealing night gown. Nonetheless she was reveling in the hapless guy's helplessness. For a moment she thought she could give in to him, but resisted the temptation. She was still obsessed with the man of her fantasies and hoping for an encounter with him before she was done with her dream vacation on the beach. She still had only one day left in the vacation.

She went around the beach hoping to meet the young man. But as the day progressed she started realizing the folly of trying to locate a person who she had seen only once and that too on a beach that had people coming in and going out by the day.

As the day ended it was time for her to pack her bags only to go back to the mundane world where to get a man to sleep with would not be that difficult; nor would it be as exciting. She tipped the bearer and thanked him for the wonderful service and promised him to come back to the same hut the next time she was on vacation. He left the place happily thanking her secretly for having given him a story for his private consumption.

As she came out of the hut and started walking away, she heard the faint call of someone through the breeze. She turned back to see a man walk briskly towards her waving his hand at her. He had something in his hand. As he came closer she was overcome by a mixed sense of relief, shyness and excitement. It was the young man with her favorite book in his hand.

What followed was a night of uninhibited indulgence in which he took her to a world of wild fantasies. For a first time in her life she was left wondering how much world was contained in the confines of the four walls of a small hut. Surprisingly she could feel her fantasy of being the girl in her favorite book coming true. She could relate the night to the stories in the book.

Lying exhausted in bed she curiously asked him if he indeed read her favorite book before returning it to her. He replied in the affirmative saying that it was his favorite book too. What he had to tell her then knocked her off her feet.

She no longer needed the book. The creator of the book was at her service.

I Never Left You

The warm wet kiss on his cheek woke him up. He opened his eyes and strained them against the bright sunlight that flowed into the room. Even without getting up from his bed he took her into his arms as she clenched him in a tight hug. He returned a kiss on her tender cheek and continued kissing her all over her angelic face. She had her artistic eyes closed as he cuddled her.

She reminded him that it was time for him to leave for work. She then gave him a list of her expectations from him for that day. He stared at her almost absentmindedly wondering if she was the same little girl who did not even know to recognize him when she was born. He wondered how she commanded his life. He gave her assurances and started off to work as she waved at him.

As he drove, his eyes moistened at the thought of his little girl. He was feeling particularly touchy that day and not without reason. It was exactly three years since his wife whom he loved so dearly left him her replica before departing to a more comfortable world. Memories bombarded his heavy heart ruthlessly. The pain was excruciating. Only he knew how he had raised the little one all those three years. But he knew that he had traveled only a very small part of the journey.

His wife departed exactly an hour after his little one was born. He did not know how to spend that peculiar day every year—it was a day of confusion for him. He had all the reason not to go to work and instead spend time with his daughter on her birthday, but deliberately avoided being home for the fear of succumbing to the conflicting emotions that ran high inside his system.

At about ten miles from home he got a jolt when a woman tried to cross over the road just in front of his car. He managed to brake the car without hurting her but in that process banged his head against the steering wheel. Fortunately for him nothing much happened. He pulled over the car by the roadside and frantically yelled at the woman almost abusively. She, by then had crossed the road and turned towards him momentarily before proceeding in her direction. Her momentary glance gave him a jitter—he thought she was smiling and she did not seem to have been startled a bit. He found it weird. His pulse was coming back to normal but the experience confounded him to the core.

The incident shook him up so badly that he started feeling insecure about his little one. Without thinking further he dropped his plans of going to work and turned his car homeward. On his way back his mind was busy processing the incident and he could sense that it had got something to do with the bigger scheme of his life, but did not know precisely what it was.

As he reached home he could feel an eerie silence outside the main door. His mind sensed something out of the usual. Heart throbbing, he opened the door silently. His vision preceded his body into the house. He was obsessed with the safety of his little daughter. Anxiety was writ on his dull face weathered by the stresses of daily life.

What he saw as he entered stunned him. The house was filled with a strange light that was as bright as his daughter's face. He called out for the babysitter who had been taking care of his daughter since the time his wife died, only to find that she was lying on the floor almost as if unconscious. He reached her and tried waking her up. She opened her eyes briefly and gave him a lovely smile that looked like the display of a great satisfaction, before slipping back into a state of unconsciousness. Unable to understand what was happening, he frenziedly called out for his daughter and headed to her room to ensure if everything was fine with her.

Though he was anxious, he felt no fear—in spite of things looking weird, surprisingly everything seemed to be boding well. He opened the door to his daughter's room and found her fast asleep. She had one of the most beautiful smiles on her face—an unadulterated smile that only children could afford.

He calmly went and sat by her side gazing into her innocent face. Unwilling to disturb her he came out of the room to check on the babysitter. As he headed out of the room he could see the babysitter walking hastily towards him. She saw him and quickly apologized to him with downcast eyes. He did not feel any resentment for her and gave her a day off. But he did issue a mild warning to her to be alert with his little one. She nodded to him thankfully and walked out hurriedly. That the babysitter was still in a sort of trance did not escape his notice—her eyes had a glow that typified a woman who achieved all she wanted in life.

Overcome with exhaustion, he lay down on the couch sipping coffee. He was trying to connect the events to make sense of what was happening to him—the woman on the road, the bright light in the house, the unconscious babysitter and his blissfully asleep daughter. He sipped his coffee and looked around to locate the source of the light but everything else looked as normal as every day. He thought he should have interrogated the babysitter.

As he closed his eyes in deep thought he could feel a hand on his shoulder. Thinking it was his daughter he slowly opened his eyes and turned his head only to see the something very spectacular, something that defied wisdom—his wife stood by his side as if trying to speak with him. Startled, he tried to wake himself up from an ostensible slumber. The more he tried to wake up the more he realized that he was awake.

In an act of coping, he sputtered something at her. He felt an uncharacteristic tightness inside his guts. His nervousness was evident. She smiled and sat beside him and as if to calm his nerves, gave him a kiss on his cheek—the same warm kiss his daughter gave him every day. She rested her head on his drooping shoulders and looked deeply into his eyes that were round with suspense. She held his shivering hand and gave a tight squeeze as if to assure him.

He was dumbfound and confused, unsure if he was indeed dreaming—but his state was definitely not that of fearfulness; it was a state of excitement and disbelief. Moments passed and he was slowly settling down but still unable to believe what was in front of his eyes. As he composed himself, he thought she asked him how he was doing. He could not take his eyes off her. She looked like an angel from the heavens and had the same innocent charm in her face that she had when they first met. He could see why he did not miss her so much; after all he had with him her exact copy—the deep brown eyes, the god-chiseled nose, the charming pout, the pink cheeks and beautiful black curls.

It was no longer a dream for him and he was sure that he indeed was sitting with his sweetheart. He sat there without uttering a word for hours that he lost count of. She too did not speak. But their hearts engaged in a silent conversation and recounted the wonderful moments they spent together. Most of the conversation was centered on their little princess and she thanked him for taking care of her well, to which he replied that she was the only purpose of his life. They spoke silently for hours before she vanished from there to the pitter-patter of nimble feet. The bright light that existed till then disappeared.

Even before he realized he saw his princess in his lap. He kissed her profusely and she did not complain about his prickly stubble.

The next day as he was driving to work he saw a woman crossing the road at a distance. He slowed down and watched her carefully. She was the same woman who almost bumped into his car the previous day. He turned his car and headed back home as if by some divine instruction.

As he entered the house he saw a bright light and the babysitter lying unconscious on the floor with a lovely smile on her face. He slowly made his way into his daughter's room. His wife was singing a lullaby and putting the little princess to sleep. Seeing him she signaled to him to be quiet. He sat down by her side silently watching the greatest possible transaction in the universe. Tears did not roll from his eyes. She kissed him and disappeared from there. The bright light disappeared too.

The babysitter apologized to him and admitted that she routinely fell asleep exactly around the time his daughter slept. She admitted that by the time she woke up, his daughter would have slept off. She further admitted that this had been happening since the time the girl was born. He smiled at her and she stood there amused.

The next day he saw the same woman crossing the road. She waved at him before disappearing to the other side of the road. He drove to work happily with a newfound confidence that he was not alone. He raised his head as if to thank the heavens and he could see his wife telling him, “I never left you dear”.

The Great Wall

He sat in the spacecraft that was ready to leave the earth. He had bought a package that covered tours to three planets and back to earth. It was exciting for him because it was always his dream to travel outside earth and explore beyond. The entire trip would take about two earth-months.

His co-passengers too seemed excited as much as he was. As the spacecraft took off and breached the earth's pulling range, he could feel changes to his physical and mental states. He found the weightlessness interesting but the sense of separation from the planet that held him so long gave him a weird feeling. As he peeped out of the window he could see the earth in her totality—round, blue, and magnificent. He was amazed by the fact that he actually lived on the same piece of astronomical wonder called earth but never learnt to appreciate her beauty. Seeing her from a distance he

knew that he missed the forest for the trees—all his years on earth he was so consumed by unnecessary detail that he did not have the time to think about the more beautiful things life offered him.

The spacecraft went from one orbit to the other having brushes with celestial objects. Seeing from the window he no longer could recognize the earth from other stars and planets. The view was breathtaking. There were patches of light in the great darkness that surrounded the spacecraft. The darkness was intimidating but somewhere it had a peculiar romantic appeal.

Gradually the infinite view of the universe started becoming monotonous and he was not enjoying it anymore. To break the tedium he turned his attention towards the interior of the spacecraft and appreciated the advances in technology that had enabled space travel.

Traveling in space, he lost sense of time and direction. After a few hours of travel there was an announcement that the spacecraft reached the first destination. It was a planet known to have inhabitants who were a race much advanced than humans, nevertheless a very helpful and a peaceful lot. They were believed to have their origins on the earth and theories existed that they shared a gene common to human beings indicating that they indeed evolved from human beings.

As the doors of the spacecraft opened for the passengers to set their foot on the planet, the tour guide announced that they had one planet-day to go around and explore. She suggested a few places and gave them some tips on how to navigate the new planet. She asked them not to worry about getting lost because the tickets tagged to their wrists were equipped with tracking devices that would help them come back to the spacecraft from anywhere on the planet.

While many of his co-passengers were forming groups and hiring the local travel modes, he decided to take a solitary walk on the planet. The roads were well laid and illuminated. Vehicles were silent and there were no emissions. There was absolute discipline everywhere. The planet looked like heaven. As he kept walking he was amazed by the planet's stark resemblance to the earth. Inhabitants looked almost similar to earthlings but had slightly larger heads indicating an intellectual evolution.

He met an old lady on one of the road crossings and struck a conversation as he walked along with her. As they parted ways he asked her for directions to what according to her were the most exciting parts of the planet. She hesitated a bit before silently pointing her finger in a certain direction. She did not speak anything and waved him good bye before disappearing into the distance. He was amused by the sudden change in the woman's demeanor and behavior towards him.

He started walking in the direction the woman pointed. He could see a gradual change in the landscape of the planet with every mile he covered walking. The structures changed their geometry, the people seemed more stoical and the breeze had a different flavor that reminded him of something that he did not know.

After walking for almost a planet-hour, he reached a huge wall that seemed to span the entire breadth of the planet. He marveled the engineering prowess that would have gone into making the wall. It seemed like the geographical limit of the planet beyond which nothing existed. There was not a single door in the wall; nor was there a window through which one could see what was on the other side. As he looked around he realized that he had walked so long that he probably reached an area of no habitation. He was alone, standing in front of an impregnable boundary that seemed to challenge his patience, intelligence and his very purpose in life.

He stared at the wall aimlessly for hours that he could not reckon, but was not tired of doing so. There was something irresistible about the wall. Gradually he could see fantastic images coming up on the wall and the images had something to tell him. They had answers to many questions he had about life. They made him understand what he was doing the right way and where he was going wrong. Almost central to all the stories on the wall was his relationship with his sweetheart, which lately was undergoing an unpleasant turbulence. He stood there for many hours imbibing the essence of the images.

Back inside the spacecraft, on his way to the next planet he started thinking deeply about the wall. Trips to the other two planets were relatively uneventful as he decided to stay back in the spacecraft. He was at his contemplative best. For almost ten years he did not find so much time to think about his relationship.

As the spacecraft started its journey back to the earth he was making a few decisions for himself. The spacecraft glided smoothly into the earth's gravitational field and he was longing to meet his sweetheart. As the earth's pull intensified, so did his longing. He could again see the earth in her magnificent blue hue.

From the space station, he rushed like a child running back home after school hours. She was not home when he reached there. He waited for her desperately for hours. Days passed and inquiries with neighbors and friends did not help trace her whereabouts. Since the time their relationship hit the wrong note he had not been bothered about what she was doing or where she went. There were times when they hardly saw each other for days together in spite of living under the same roof.

At a time when his desperation for her transformed into hopelessness, one morning he woke up to a knock on the door. He was in for a pleasant surprise to find his darling standing by. She seemed like consumed by a sense of urgency—an urgency to meet him. She breezed in and kissed him passionately. Within no time they found themselves in a complete union and not a single piece of cloth dared to come in between them for the fear of being burnt by the passion. It was almost after a year that they found themselves in such an intimate situation. He gave in to the passion wondering silently about the fact that she was in a reconciliatory mood obviating the need for him to make the first move of reconciliation. None of them uttered a word about the past but they resolved to bury the hatchet.

For the rest of their fulfilling lives both of them did not know that they were standing on the opposite sides of the same great wall precisely at the same time when a realization occurred to them. Both of them thanked the old woman for directing them to the wall even as she was busy showing another earthling the way to the great wall—a wall called ego—a magnificent creation of the human mind.

And The Gods Of Love Retired

Her feminine scent drove him crazy and wild. She looked as ravishing as ever in her figure hugging designer jeans. But it was only a matter of time before her dress found its place in the heap of irrelevant clothing that lay inanimate on a romantically designed floor. She was equally consumed by his animal magnetism as she started exploring him unrelentingly.

The bed delightfully bore the burden of their creative performance. The scene was akin to a laboratory where new hypotheses of love-making were being postulated and proved. They were both teaching each other and also learning at the same time. Goddesses and gods of love seemed to be making notes about the new experimental findings and were disappointed to realize how outdated their prescriptions were. Conventional beliefs and theories were getting disproved. New centers of pleasure in the human body and mind were being

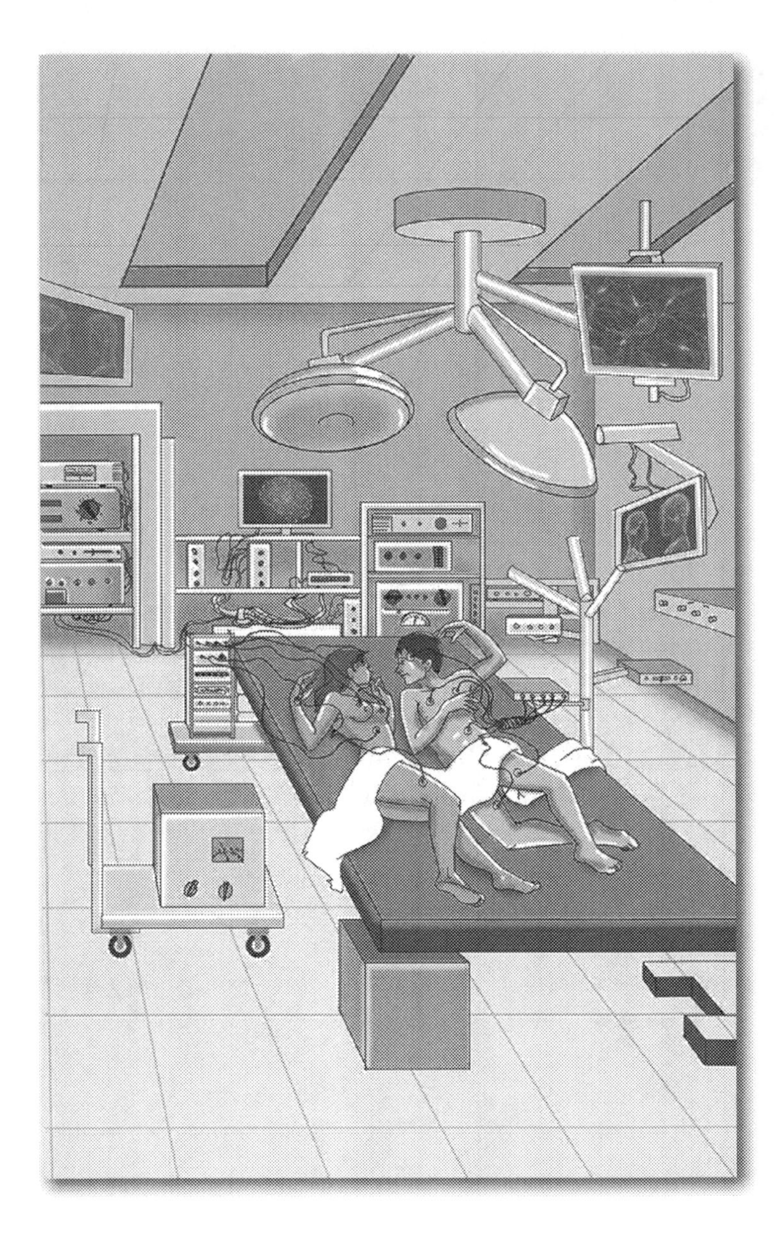

identified. Sometimes the bed, sometimes the floor, sometimes the wall—the center of action kept shifting but the spirit was intact. Logical barriers were being broken and it seemed like another step in the evolution of humankind. Cameras mounted on the walls and attached to the cot were happily recording away the deific phenomenon and did not blink for a moment. Unsated, the couple wanted more but hit the limits of physical endurance.

They sat on the bed looking at each other admiringly. As the hormonal balance in their bodies was getting restored they carefully started removing the little transducers and sensors that were embedded in great numbers across their bodies. She kissed him passionately on his lips and asked him huskily when the next round of experiments would be, to which he replied that it would be very soon.

Sitting on his chair he was busy analyzing the various graphs that were the result of the exercise the previous night. He was playing back the tape that had the recording of the event and correlating the frames with the graphs. After endless sessions of experimentation he was in the final stages of his research. He was amazed by the findings of his own research and found it hard to believe some of them. He was in astonishment about the mounds of data that a year of interaction between a woman and a man can yield.

As he was typing a report, she walked in and stood beside him silently. She cleared her throat as if to announce her arrival. He raised his head and looked at her. She appeared quite normal and did not have on her face even the slightest trace of the effects of their exploits the previous night. He gestured to her to wait as he hurriedly typed into his computer.

He made her sit and started to plan for another round of experimentation. She was all ears for him and absorbed the plan without showing up any kind of emotion, intervening only sparingly with her own ideas. He wondered if she was the same diva that assisted him in his experiments. He could see two personalities of her—one of a dispassionate professional and the other of a highly emotional being who knew to tug at the right strings at the right time. As they finished the planning for that night, he hesitatingly asked her what she thought about a proposal he placed with her some time ago. She gave a disapproving nod and walked out of the room as casually as she came in. He was disappointed but quickly composed himself back into his work. He resumed playing the tape and played it over and over. There was an inexplicable beauty in her eyes, in her body and in her mind. He gently slid into the memories when he hired her as a subject for his research.

He remembered the day she came for an interview at his office. She had a raw unexploited charm about her. By that time he had already interviewed a few other girls but either he was not satisfied with them or they found the job too unorthodox. But this girl patiently listened to the job description and agreed to all the terms without the slightest hesitation. He pre-warned her about the perils—both the physical and the psychological—that such a job would entail but she did not show any reluctance. The first of the experimentation series was a very nervous affair for him but she did not display any edginess. That which started off as a simple interaction between them evolved into a series of experiments that involved unconventional methods—some of them posing an apparent danger to their wellbeing. But neither of them budged. He always speculated about the reasons for her loyalty to him or her passion for the experiments. He knew it was not the money because he always regretted his inability to compensate her fairly for the great efforts she was putting in. Having exposure to studies of psychology and human behavior, he knew well that she had a high emotional quotient and could not be pervert. He tried probing her personal life to understand if she needed the job out of a compulsion but understood through others that she was well-off and in fact kept herself busy with a lot of life enriching work outside office.

He was nudged back into the present by the jarring sound of the phone on his desk. As he spoke, his face had an afterglow. He was ecstatic that the topic of his dissertation got selected for a presentation in one of the most respected forums of psychological studies. He knew that he had to be really quick to complete his work well ahead of the day of presentation. He thanked himself for having been aggressive with his work and thanked his favorite subject for her unflinching commitment to the project.

The next day she walked into the experimentation chamber as usual and as per plan. He was already waiting for her. As she came in he kissed her on her forehead and announced to her about the presentation. She kissed him back and congratulated him on the achievement.

The last session of the experimentation started as planned. Both of them drank a potion that he had specially brewed after reading a lot of ancient literature. The potion was supposed to have a mood-enhancing effect on the human body. Non-intruding transducers and sensors adorned their bodies as the hapless clothes on the floor grudged in resentment. The potion started showing its effect on their minds. As the game began the cameras seemed to be watching in bewilderment the proceedings in the room. Nevertheless they went about doing their work without stopping. Later, as he played back the tape to complete the dissertation he could feel his core disturbed and it was evident through the trickle of tears in his eyes. But he knew that he found a great insight for his dissertation and that insight would have a game-changing impact on psychological research.

The day of the presentation came. He ensured arrangements for her travel and ordered her to be present at the venue. She reluctantly agreed. As his turn to present was announced, he walked graciously onto the dais and flashed the presentation of his thesis onto the huge screen. After thirty minutes of spellbinding presentation of his observations, analysis and recommendations, the audience rose to their feet applauding and acknowledging his brilliance as she watched him silently without displaying on her face any emotions. Oblivious of the recognition from the audience, he kept staring at her and could see in her face a calm sense of great achievement. As the applause subsided, he bowed in reverence and introduced her to the audience as his research partner. Another round of applause rang through her ears exalting her respect and regard for him. She blushed for the first time in her association with him. He could sense the faint redness in her cheeks even from at a distance. He then made an announcement to the crowd that left her speechless and motionless. Through the uproar created by encouraging claps he walked to her, kissed her passionately and proposed to her as the crowd waited anxiously for her response. Moments of suspense later, she nodded almost involuntarily and the crowd erupted in joy.

Sensors and transducers now were relegated to a corner cupboard. Getting crushed in an unadorned embrace, she asked him how he garnered the courage to propose to her under the full gaze of a thousand people especially when she had spurned his proposal earlier. He just smiled at her and left the answer to her imagination.

What she did not know and could not imagine was that he had secretly destroyed the tape in which she emotionally vented out her beautiful feelings for him under the influence of the potion she drank before the last session of experimentation. What she did not remember was that they did not even touch each other during the session. What she did not know was that the secret admiration she had for him all the while was no longer a secret. She only knew that she accepted his latest proposal because it carried in it the power of a great conviction.

The cameras now retired after serving the most fruitful purpose of their existence. She playfully gave him an illegitimate squeeze when he asked her if he had to hire another assistant to keep his experimentation going. He moaned in sweet pleasure. Gods and goddesses of love were contemplating retirement too.

The Gods Of Love Retired (Part 2)

The dulcet melody of a romantic song filled the air that smelt of an impending rain. The breeze was cool and carried with it a soothing aroma from the woods that laced the mountains. The overcast sky made noon look like an evening. From an altitude where probably only gods lived, the scenery around looked like an abstruse work of a connoisseur of nature. The front yard of the cottage was beautifully set up and had a rustic charm to it. Innumerable cups of rejuvenating herbal tea warmed up his heart as much as they ignited his imagination.

His hand was moving very fast. She unmindfully stood in front of him, oblivious of what he was up to. But he knew that his inspiration came from her. At the end of a long session, he let out a sigh of relief as if to signal the end of an assignment and settled down in the teakwood sofa. She looked at him to see if she now could ease

herself a bit. Getting a nod of approval from him she just came and collapsed beside him in the sofa.

They both sat for many moments staring at her portrait that he just created. She felt flattered and the more she looked at her own portrait the more she fell in love with him and with herself. She could not contain her appreciation for him and asked him dreamily, "Why did you not tell me all these years about the artist hidden inside you? It is unfair on your part to have hidden such a wonderful talent from your partner for life." Her pout indicated a certain degree of benign annoyance. Her eyes were expressions of combined emotions of appreciation, love and shyness that were brought about by a sense of self-discovery. He filliped her on her cheek and whispered in her ear, "I never hid anything from you. In fact all these years the artist's hands were busy doing something else. Today the manifestation was different." His hands slid suggestively. She blushed. They united and it was the portrait's turn to blush.

Many moments later, the laden clouds let out an orgasmic burst and seemed to be floating away delightfully. The sun appeared hurriedly onto the scene as if to catch a glimpse even as he lightened up the mountains with his life-giving rays.

As dusk fell on the mountains that till then gleamed in the light of the afternoon sun, the old care-taker of the cottage switched on the lamps that were charged by the sun through the day. He had a stoic look on his face that belied his strong sense of appreciation for the couple. He kept looking at the portrait only to be brought back to his senses to a question the couple had. He nodded and told them about a beautiful place a few miles to the east of their cottage. The night passed by quite eventfully for the couple. The rarefied air of the high mountains seemed to be working in their favor as it meant only a thinner film separating their bodies.

The next day morning they did not have to wake up. The tiredness that was the result of a completely sleepless night did not deter them from embarking on a trip to the spot the caretaker had suggested. As they started walking the caretaker saw them off. He had something to tell them but they were not in a mood to listen. He shook his head disapprovingly.

They reached the spot as the sun was just rising on the mountains. It was a fantastic view and they were lost in the beauty that nature seemed to have painstakingly created. They sat on a ridge with a feeling of being pleasantly lost. Their tiredness no longer bothered them. The breeze was as cool as they were hot the previous day.

They sat there for hours, soaking in the warm sun and being tempered by the cool breeze. He looked at her and could see a different kind of glow in her face. She looked at him and saw calmness in his face that she never saw in all the years of their relationship.

Hours later they both got up and started walking along the ridge feeling amazed by the depth the valley offered. The valley seemed to contain in it more secrets than their hearts could hold at a time. The hide and seek the sun was playing behind the clouds did not seem to bother the couple. They lost the reckoning of how far they walked only to be stopped by a beautiful water body. It looked like a pond but was only slightly bigger than a puddle. The water was blue, but had tinges of brownishness attributed to it by the rocky surroundings. Dispersed across the pond were lovely lotuses of varied colors. Most lovely of the lotuses were the red ones that looked very vibrant.

They stood there fixated on the beauty of the pond. The pond seemed to be arousing feelings of great love in the couple. They both got a naughty thought almost at the same time. He looked at her adoringly and held her hand in his. Seizing on her, he kissed her passionately on her lips that were as red as the lotuses in the pond. She closed her eyes as if in imagination. The lip-lock continued for some time and her hands were getting busy. Who removed whose clothes was inconsequential, as the outcome was a completely nature-clad pair of beautiful lovers. His muscles were as strong as the mountains while her womanly endowments reminded of peaks and valleys. He bent his knees and lifted her into his arms as she put her hand gracefully around his neck. He walked slowly towards the pond and gently placed her in the water. They swam to the middle of the pond and stood there hugging each other almost neck deep in water. Below and above the surface of the cool and crisp water, their bodies corresponded in unison as they continued to take advantage of the buoyancy offered by the water. The lotuses kept swaying to the love ripples.

The pond regained its original calmness as the couple lay floating on their backs. But the water had something in it that was meddling with the minds of the couple. He broke the ice first and a serious conversation ensued. The conversation went on and on till the sun reached his zenith. As they waded themselves out of the pond there was an express contentment on their faces and their hearts shed the burden created by the hypnotic effect of the water.

Once out of the pond they dressed up and started walking back to the cottage. She looked at him dotingly and he gave it back to her with innumerable kisses all the way through.

They reached the cottage as the sun was setting. As they walked in, they were greeted by the caretaker who just started lighting the lamps. His thick moustache could not hide his anxiety. Glancing sideways at them he tried to judge their situation. Their wet hair hinted to him that they played in water. It could not be rain because it did not rain that day. He took a quick order from them for their evening dinner and disappeared into the kitchen. Preparing dinner, he eavesdropped on the conversation the couple was having. Though his age and wisdom warned him that it was not proper, the same age and wisdom authorized him to snoop into their conversation—he was genuinely concerned for them.

As he served them dinner, the conversation the couple just had kept ringing in his mind. He thought to himself as telling them, "My children, the pond that you just got in is not an ordinary pond. It has the reputation of having been blessed and cursed at the same time by the gods of love ages ago. Anyone getting into the pond cannot hide one's feelings for others. Even the secretly guarded feelings are dragged out under the influence of the water. I am happy that you have come out with your relationship unscathed. In fact you seem to be more in love with each other now than when you came here."

What the old man did not know was that the couple indeed was the gods of love who blessed the pond eons ago.

The Divine Game of Chance

(A story in six chapters)

Chapter Six

The Beginning

He could no longer bear the deafening silence that shrouded the bedroom. He always believed that any differences between a wife and a husband are best left at the threshold of the bedroom; on the bed side of the threshold there could be only one soul albeit in two bodies—at least when the two bodies were not in fusion. But she lay on the bed as if she was some other soul that he could not relate to. It was not too uncommon for them to have carried some of their clashes into the bedroom, but every such incident looked so new and unique to him that he could seldom use his experience to resolve a problem at hand. But most often an issue would get resolved as if the gods of love returned from a short break to mend the situation. It was just that the duration of the break varied from time to time and from problem to problem—sometimes it was a matter of a couple of days and at other times a matter of a few seconds.

He broke the silence first as a god of love shot his naughty but mighty arrow at him. "Dear! I don't think I have made a mistake. Your silence makes me jittery. Tell me if there is something I can do to make you happy. At least I should know what is bothering you." She looked at him intensely. But behind the intensity he could sense some confusion and tiredness. He knew she was tired but he wanted her to tell him that she was exhausted. It was then when a sweet arrow stung her, "You know what! It is all because of you and your two kids. You have made my life miserable." Behind her made-up furiousness he could see a clear and unalloyed innocence. "What did the kids or I do to make you unhappy?" She replied with multiplied innocence, "Your kids are giving me sleepless nights. I do not have time left to think about myself. I am tired." He now knew that she was giving in, "I understand dear. It is but a passing phase. It is only a matter of time that the younger one will stand on his own two feet. You will have a plenty of time left for yourself and will keep wondering what to do with all the time." He held her hand gently and gave her a passionate kiss on her pink lips, "And you just said that they were my kids. Are they not your kids too?" he winked at her. She displayed her situational pout, "They are your kids, and I just bore them for you. I was not even sure when you seeded them inside me. It is all because of you that I am having sleepless nights." Now he knew that she was getting naughty because he knew how much she loved the kids. He said, "Now that the kids are fast asleep, do you mind another sleepless night?"

Chapter Five

The Naughty Angel

The sleepless night indeed began. His intensity made her pleasantly worried lest she should have to bear another child by accident. She did not want more sleepless nights—she knew that her sleepless nights were his too and she was more concerned about him than about herself. Nevertheless she was enjoying the sleeplessness as much as he was.

As the night progressed with him and her becoming one soul and one body, they both remembered the days before their second child was born. A virtual time machine magically transported them three years into the past.

"I have some news for you," she said with a twinkle in her eyes that seemed to be dominating her face that was already glowing for some reason. "Don't tell me that we have another angel coming our way," trying to recollect the last time the gods of love played their big role. She nodded in excitement. He found himself suddenly consumed by an instinctive ecstasy. He kissed her profusely and slipped into her warm embrace.

Many days later—"Is it a girl or a boy?" both exclaimed silently as he felt his hand about her heavily pregnant belly. Two more months to the due date and it felt like an eternity. "How does it matter if it is a boy or a girl!" her eyes seemed to express. "I share your feeling," he conveyed through his sleepy eyes. The kick from within assured them of a healthy progress especially in the backdrop of a certain ordeal they had to endure almost four years ago. He counted the number of kicks and checked his observation against the recommendation in his favorite website on pregnancy and childbirth. He literally lost count of the times he referred to the same website. But he kept on going back to reassure himself that all was well. He felt her heavy breathing that was purportedly because of the pressure created by a new life on her internal organs. But even before he could say something to her he realized that she was already fast asleep as if unmindful of his anxiety about the wellbeing of the mother-life and the new-life. He closed his eyes with his hand still placed gently on her bulge and feeling the kicks. Without realizing that she, by virtue of being a woman, inherently had a far more superior instinct than his, he wondered how she could sleep so peacefully.

Days passed by. But somehow he felt that time elongated infinitely. He gave in to his limited and layman understanding of the theory of relativity—'the length of time varies according to the frame of reference'—time that used to fly earlier was now barely crawling. It reminded him of his childhood when he hated waiting on a railway platform for a train that was running indefinitely behind schedule. Every minute was a heavy minute. He did not sleep peacefully for all those days and was on a ridiculously zealous alert that he himself never considered ridiculous. She understood his concern and was happy that she had such a wonderful man to take care of her, but at the same time had mild pangs of irritation about being pampered to the extent that he often ignored many of her assurances.

Two months later that took an eternity to pass by, one fine morning she complained sheepishly of a characteristic uneasiness. She was not sure though if it were indeed a false alarm. He swung into action and as was his wont, hauled her to the doctor's office without the slightest premeditation. His action proved to be not without a basis. The doctor ordered for an immediate admission.

A literally laborious process began. Minutes looked like hours and hours sounded like days. He stood beside her in the room with a helpless yet hopeful look on his face trying to give her the confidence that she could actually do it. But her situation was akin to a pendulum—oscillating between one extreme of the tremendous effort of labor and the other extreme of unconsciousness. The midwives kept exhorting her through traditional means that combined encouragement and coercion. The little life inside was so attached to its mother that it refused to come out. It was like a naughty prank the gods of love were playing. But all she knew was that she had her hand firmly in his hand and that was all that mattered to her at that time.

He had his gaze fixed on a monitor that sounded like a horse galloping through rocky terrains. He knew it was his heartbeat that was emanating from her body. The monitor indicated occasional breaches in the acceptable thresholds of heartbeat. The usually composed midwives and the doctor now looked a bit rattled.

The smell of a drizzle that crept in from the ventilator and the pleasant songs of birds outside made their alert but worn out minds wander with striking coincidence into the past when their "first" one arrived. The gods of love watched the show in amusement as if unaware of the potential outcome of their naughty experiments on their subjects.

Chapter Four

The Beautiful Angel

"Why should it happen only to me? What misdeed am I paying the price for?"

Tears rolled down profusely through her sunken eyes onto her cheeks chafed with incessant crying. He held her hand firmly and hugged her with all the firmness that was just insufficient to comfort her. His broad shoulders and manly physique did not correlate with the trickle in his eyes. Tears from the two sets of emotion-ravaged eyes fused seamlessly as if to reflect the same story of anguish that they shared.

Father Time, for all his healing powers failed to heal their wounds completely. But their resilience and approach to life enthused the gods of love resume their cosmic act. Invisible arrows abounded the romantic environment he set up to enable her overcome the past and in that process to repair his own damaged heart that was indeed hers. But now, the overtures and bedroom transactions had a business like tone that was intended to make good an earlier loss.

The day of reckoning arrived and she indifferently told him that she was pregnant. He was a personification of mixed feelings of happiness, anxiety, apathy and confusion. He kissed her intuitively—the passion that was once a common trait between them was conspicuous by its absence. But she knew that his love for her was intact and was unconditional. She had a promise to deliver and that made her grittier than what she originally was.

Endless errands to the doctor's office frustrated the doctor but not them. They felt as if caught in a time warp characterized by a giant clock that had the seconds hand moving at the pace of its hour hand. For a first time in his life he could sense the weight of time.

Technology helped them with assurances only to a certain extent. "I wish how women had telltale indicators on their tummies. How I wish I could just open the shutters and have a quick peek to see what goes on inside," he remarked sometime after the supposed halfway milestone of an arduous journey. She simply smiled back at his apparently childlike remark. The radiant smile was that of a supreme confidence that everything was going to be fine and did not have an iota of sarcasm in it. Nonetheless she was more concerned about his psychotic illusions and imaginations that were probably the result of the many sleepless nights he was having. She counseled him not to stress himself out with too much research and tried convincing him that she knew well about what was happening inside her. But any amount of assurance could not calm his nerves. She went back to her serene sleep mode because she knew she had to take care not only of herself but also of a new promise that was growing within her.

He lay down beside her with his hand feeling the movements within her body and his mind doing some math. Slowly but steadily his eyelids dropped as if pulled down by a ton. There was a dream that was trying to come into his sleep—in fact there were not one, but many dreams that were hitting his sleep sphere. From among the mélange of incoherent visions that generally ranged from meaningless dreams to nightmares there emerged a rare scene in which he saw a huge ocean that looked like milk. There were no waves, but the continuous ripples had a mesmerizing appeal. They appeared to be able to tell him about his past, his present and his future. Suddenly the ripples stopped and the ocean looked like a vast lake of some veritable ambrosia. Little angels with wafer-thin wings circled the lake with tiny bows and arrows in their hands. They looked like the progeny of the gods of love. From the placid lake emerged little bubbles that burst softly and from within appeared zillions of lively and life-inspiring creatures that looked strange but very beautiful. They were all jumping in a playful mood and emanating music like noise that filled his heart with warmth and inexplicable happiness.

She woke him up. "What were you dreaming about that made you smile so much?" she asked him eagerly. She was curious to know all about the dream that made him smile almost after a year. "I am seeing a god of love entering our lives," he replied vaguely and slithered back into deep sleep almost instantly. She kept looking at his face that looked so different. She was amused but was happy for him at the same time.

The big day arrived. It was in the early hours that she lay under the gaze of specialists and expert nurses. Waiting outside the labor room he could hear the rhythmic sounds coming from the heart monitor. The rhythm matched his pace as he walked up and down the aisle restlessly.

He kept issuing a lot of positive messages to himself but the specter of a dreadful situation precisely a year ago loomed large. The wait was excruciating. His head was breaking from the pressure created by his brain that probably would have looked like a cobweb studded with diamonds—the cobweb indicating the fear of the repeat of an untoward event and the diamonds, his hope.

The smell of a drizzle and the pleasant songs of birds outside made his alert but worn out mind wander into the past when their "original first" did not arrive. The gods of love watched the show in silence as his mind moved slowly into the past.

Chapter Three

The Angel That Did Not Arrive

"What a nightmare it was!" he exclaimed to her as he came staggering out of the bedroom. He looked extremely tensed and visibly shaken. She stopped preparing the morning coffee and kissed his forehead that was wet with droplets of sweat. Concerned, she asked him, "Take it easy dear. What's the matter?" He did not speak for a while and just collapsed into the chair. She knew that it was very uncharacteristic of him to behave the way he did that day.

"I saw a gory dream and I cannot tell you how horrifying it was. Never saw such a dream in my life [sic]," he said trying to compose himself. She comforted him by giving him a hug, "Don't worry dear and take it easy. Tell me what you saw." After a long pause he narrated to her the entire dream. Though she tried cheering him up by acting romantic, she too was shaken by what she heard from him.

The nightmare lingered in his memory for the days to come but faded into obscurity as more days passed by.

It was a pleasant evening. Both of them sat in the verandah sipping tea and looking into each other's eyes as if they had nothing else to do. A slight drizzle started and the smell of the wet soil brought back nostalgic memories. As if by some reciprocal arrangement both of them found the setting extremely romantic. Being newly married, they found the growing passion irresistible. Arrows of love hormones came from nowhere to create a sweet pain in their hearts. They did not need a bed. He planted his seed in her field. A ripe fruit dropped off a tree symbolizing something, even as she dozed off from the exhaustion induced by the intense game. The gods of love wore a fazed look on their faces as they realized that their arrows were ill-timed. She woke up jolted.

A day came that was going to change their lives forever. As he came back home from work that evening she was already waiting restlessly for him. As soon as he came in she ran towards him, hugged him and kissed him on his lips. He was surprised to see the change in her behavior and suspected a genuinely strong reason. She pointed her finger towards her abdomen and whispered huskily into his ears, "I checked with the doctor and we will very soon have a little one pitter-pattering all over the house." His heart erupted in joy and she became a privileged victim of his strong embrace. As they were lost in their world of fantasies and dreams, little did they realize that they had embarked on a beautiful journey that would lead them to nowhere. The gods of love were feeling guilty.

Many months later the nightmares they saw came true and there was neither a drizzle nor was there the music of songbirds. Torrents of tears replaced the drizzle and sobs, the music. The gods of love too shed a divine tear.

Chapter Two

Connecting the Dots

A sudden shrill cry woke him up from the sad recollection of a tragedy. "Congratulations sir," came out the midwife and hurriedly went back into the labor room after collecting something that he was not bothered about.

"Both the mother and the baby are fine," said the doctor. The midwife brought with her a cute thing wrapped carefully in a piece of soft cloth and placed it gently into his hands. Hands shivering, he held the baby and apprehensively looked at its eyes unable to believe the truth that was in front of him. A sudden wriggle inside the wrapper assured him of a reality that he was still finding difficult to believe. The midwife exclaimed softly as if not to disturb the mirthfully asleep bundle of new life, "He is a beautiful angel. Sir, seeing the little one I can be very sure of the love you have for your wife." He felt flattered, but the sense of holding his bundle of joy was more overwhelming. More than that, he felt as if woken up from a nightmare to the most beautiful thing in their life. The midwife kept giving him tips about how to take care of the kid during the initial period. But slowly the entire scene faded in front of his eyes and a new scene emerged in which he realized that her hand still held his firmly and he was in fact inside the labor room along with his wife. The monitor no longer showed any heartbeat. She was in a state of semi-consciousness. As he tried to come back to senses and figure out what was happening he remembered that he smelt a drizzle and heard the pleasant songs of the birds outside before he slipped into a dream. "Congratulations," said the midwife, "both the baby and the mother are fine. But I must tell you sir, this fellow is a naughty angel—he would not come out of his mother's body and I must compliment you for your patience. I have not seen a father spend such a long time inside the labor room," and she placed the naughty angel in his hands.

Outside the labor room they both were doting on the new bundle of joy. He looked at her adoringly. He looked at the elder one who was extracting some big-brotherly thrills playing blissfully with the little one and the little one seemed to wink naughtily.

Chapter One

The End

They both coincidentally woke up from the entire dream sequence in which their minds played a little trick on them and enacted a complete series of life events even as they lay exhausted from a passionate exercise of love. He looked at her. His eyes seemed to be asking, "Are they not your kids too?" and she replied, "Of course, they are more mine than yours! They are my angels."

The gods of love left their representatives on the earth in the form of a beautiful angel and a naughty angel. Having accomplished their task, the gods decided to go back to their worlds and retire peacefully. The angel that did not arrive on this planet went back to her world along with the gods of love.

Gods of Love Want to Dream

(A series of improbable, but true dreams)

Introduction

"**I** dreamt of you last night," he whispered in her ear as the mild feminine scent from her hair created a romantic feeling inside him. "Why did you have to dream about me, when I am always with you?" she questioned with as assumed innocence that was to cover up the feeling of being flattered, "and what was I doing in the dream?" she asked nonchalantly, trying hard not to expose her curiosity.

"Here is the deal. I will tell you what you did in my dream, but you will have to promise me to turn it into a reality." The twinkle in his eye meant naughtiness and she knew that. She loved the way he always spiced up the bed. Every time he would come up with a novel way to keep their relationship of many years young and interesting. She replied excitingly, "Consider it a done deal!" Now the twinkle in her eye made her intentions evident to him.

"Alright," he said and started narrating the dream. She blushed at the thought of turning that dream into reality. She was all ears for him and could feel her love juices erupting uncontrollably. She was awed by his creativity and secretly worried about the feasibility of enacting some of his wild imaginations. But her ecstasy outweighed her apprehensions as the story unfurled.

She was so consumed by the narrative that she started implementing it with the fervor of a love goddess. As the dream progressed she found herself shedding her mental inhibitions as much as her sartorial hindrances in a trance like manner. He was narrating and she was enacting.

The gods and goddesses of love giggled as they watched the couple struggle sweetly with acts that they were not used to. And a dream came true. And thus began the 'dialogue of dreams'.

A Horse to Ride

"Today I will tell you the dream I saw last night," she said, tying a black cloth across his eyes. He found her act very interesting. "Is this what you saw in your dream," he asked referring to the blindfold. "Shhh!" she placed her index finger across his lips and pushed him back on the bed. Running her hands across his hairy chest, she sat astride his legs. Feeling his strong abdomen hardened by years of a natural exercise that she assisted him with, she gave him a mild tickle. From behind the blindfold across his eyes he could visualize that she was now getting her clothes off her body—the body that she considered her temple and took utmost care of. Though he could not see her, he could feel the glow of the body by the touch of his hand. She was smooth and warm.

Massaging his body from the chest to the point that his body fused with hers, she started narrating her wild dream, "Last night I was particularly feeling very tired. No sooner did I hit the bed than I fell asleep. You were telling me something but I do not remember any bit of what you said. But I did barely hear you mention the horse race you had put money in.

"I was walking alone in a vast land that was green with lots of plants that were waist high. The plants had some very peculiar leaves and the flowers looked pregnant ready to fructify. All of a sudden the entire landscape became very plain as the plants disappeared. Somehow the change in the scenario did not bother me. From a distance I could hear the hooves of a galloping horse and my mind was excited to catch of glimpse of him. I could see him come dashing towards me. As he approached me the clothes on my body started peeling off one after the other even without my intervention and I found myself clad by the beatific nature that surrounded me from all possible directions. That seemed to be the most blissful moment of my life.

"The next moment, an unsaddled and unbridled horse that was as naked as I was, stood beside me magnificently. He looked like he was inviting me to mount him, which I did with surprising élan as if I had a great experience dealing with horses. He took off at a great speed and traveled across the giant plains as I hugged him tightly by his strong neck. The wonderful rhythm with which he was galloping created an astounding resonance in some soft corners of my body that were being tickled by his shining skin laced with silken hair."

She paused to gauge the mood of her man who was lying blindfolded on the bed with his thighs getting crushed between hers. His breath was heavy and body warm. She knew by his other parameters that he was intensely aroused. "Why did you pause? What happened next?" he asked, unable to hide his curiosity and impatience.

She slowly took the blindfold off his eyes. The view he got of her could have knocked him off his feet but for a strong clamp like hold she had on him. He looked at her ravishing figure and raised his hands to clench her slim waist as if to adjust her position relative to his. She did her bit to assist him. She stooped down to kiss him on his lips and managed to align her entire body with his. He could feel the warm wetness of her tender lips. "Did you ask me what happened next in my dream?" she asked him huskily and continued, "The horse aroused me and vanished into the horizon. I did not realize when I got off his back, but the next moment I was riding you—just like this." The boldness had a playful punch in it and he always loved it when she did it.

Their bodies resonated and the gods of love were happily enjoying the ride.

The Beautiful Petals

Even before the effects of the intense love-making of previous day were gone, they both found themselves in a romantic mood. They were cozying up to each other in a couch in the verandah. "What are you searching for?" she asked impishly as his hands and fingers got busy exploring her feminine secrets.

"I saw a dream last night," he said and continued, "and in that dream I saw some very beautiful flowers." The very mention of flowers brought up a smile on her face, as she knew the mischief he was up to.

He continued, "The flowers were of varied colors but were almost similar in appearance. They looked like a hybrid between lotuses and sunflowers. The petals looked enticing in their multitude of colors. The flowers were swaying gently to the southerly breeze. I was walking through a huge field that was covered with the flower plants.

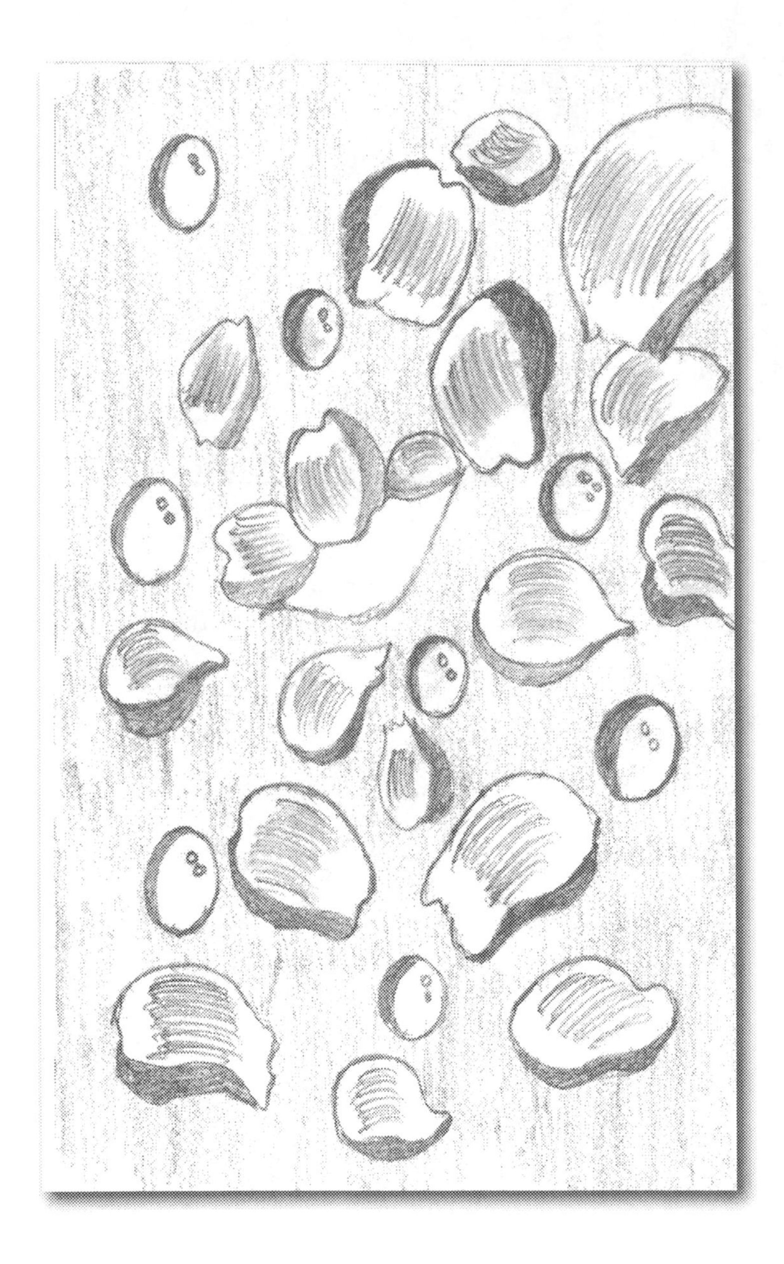

"All of a sudden the breeze changed its direction and I could hear a faint buzz in the air. The buzz started approaching me and I was looking skyward to understand where it was coming from. I could see in my dream a huge swarm of some strange objects descending on the garden. Upon close examination the objects looked familiar to me– they looked like tiny replicas of me. Each of them carefully picked a flower to settle down. As the objects settled down on the flowers the petals started closing up, literally sucking in the objects into the flowers."

As he narrated the dream, she listened to him with rapt attention and her tongue rolling over her lower lip—a characteristic sign that she was getting smitten.

His continued his narrative, "That was not all. Each time the petals closed up I could feel an inexplicable pleasure in my heart. As I waded through the field of these exotic flowers I started to see that the petals resembled your beautiful lips in the way they opened and closed."

She gave him an infatuated look and whispered something secretly in his ears. "Is this how you felt when the flowers were sucking you in?" she murmured as she held his ear between her petal lips and leaving her crude love bites. She continued her irresistible seduction, "May be I could show you what more my petals can do." She went into an amorous overdrive disclosing her innate instincts.

As her petals opened and closed tugging his masculine secrets, it was his turn to ask her, "What are you searching for?" The gods and goddess of love were lost in their own world of godly dreams.

'Many Me'

"I think I overslept." The beauty of her dark eyes got accentuated by the freshness of her face that was the result of a sound sleep. Handing over the morning coffee that he freshly brewed while she was still asleep, he looked into her eyes. The eyes seemed to be telling the story of a lovely dream she probably saw the night before. He prodded her to tell him all about that dream. Sipping the fresh brew she started speaking as if lost in deep thought and reminiscing with great fondness the dream that kept her busy through the night.

"I was walking on a road sometime in the twilight hours. I was all alone and could see a ball of red color sinking into the horizon. A bright white ball emerged from the other direction and the view was awesome. There was no need for any street lamps, and there were none anyway.

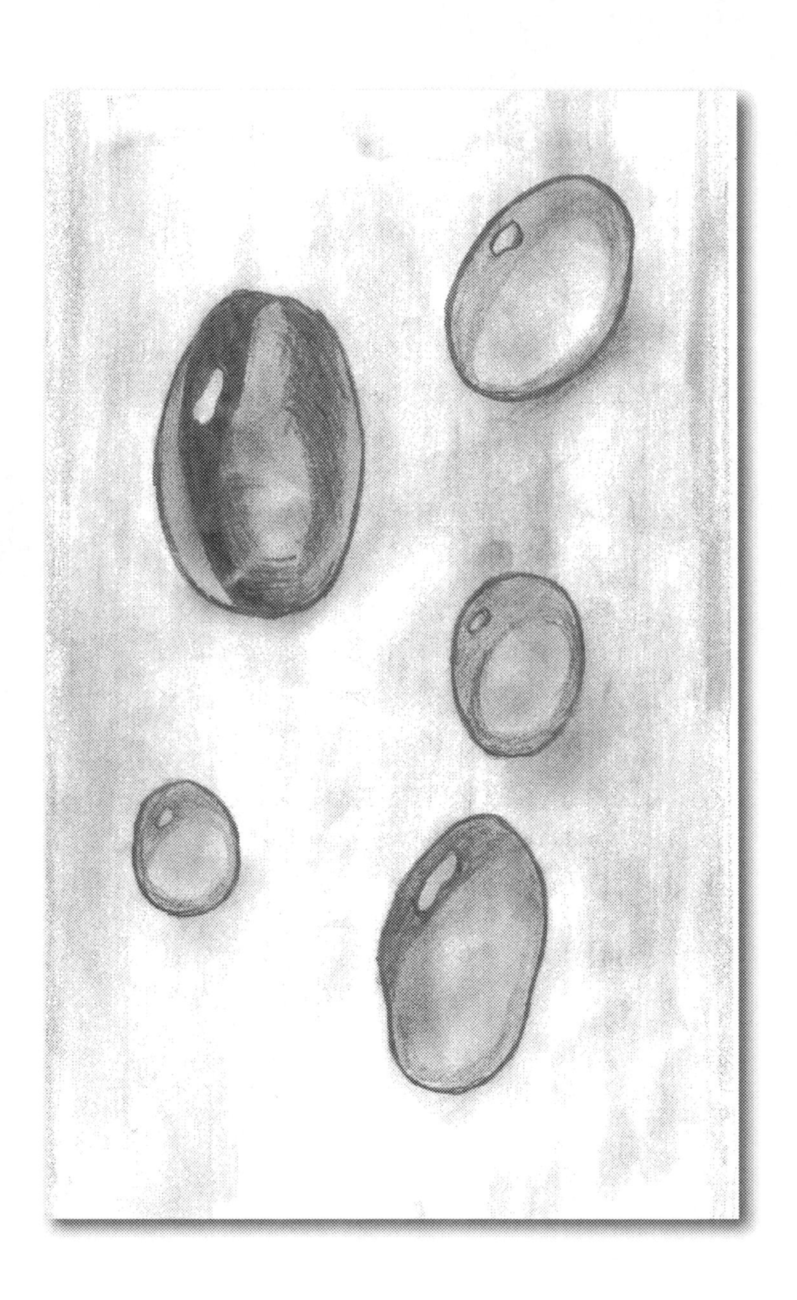

"I do not know how long I walked, but the walk was absolutely enjoyable and I did not feel an inch of tiredness. As I walked I heard something approaching me. I heard the ringing sound of a bell behind me and thought it to be a bicycle. I casually looked back and was surprised to see that it was actually a chariot that was approaching me. The chariot was driven by some beautiful creatures that looked absolutely pleasing to the mind. I stepped aside as if to give way to the chariot. But the chariot stopped gently by my side and as if by some magic I found myself getting on to it.

"Even before I could settle down in my seat the chariot took off into the air and flew like a mighty bird in the moonlit sky. It seemed to be traveling through the stars at lightning speed. It crossed many stars before finally slowing down to land on a planet that looked beautiful and blue from a distance. After hovering for a while the chariot finally landed on the planet.

"I got down and saw a group of beautiful women approaching me with garlands of flowers in their hands. Without uttering a word they bowed to me as if I were their mistress. One of the women held my hand gently and guided me to walk in the direction of a bright light that emerged from a distance. As she touched me I could feel a strange tickling sensation somewhere in my heart. For a moment I thought I was in love with her. I did not feel odd about being in love with a woman.

"As we walked through the wonderland I could feel the smell of love in the air. It was not air; it was something else. I could see a lot of couples indulge in love making openly and without inhibitions. The sight was very inspiring and roused me to the core. I asked one of my escorts if this was a common feature on the planet, to which she smiled and told me that it was a special day where all restrictions and restraints were relaxed and everyone on the planet was free to do whatever one wanted. It was a day when inhibitions were to be put on the backburner. I then asked her if it was her day of no inhibitions too. Without a trace of shyness on her face she replied that she was to meet her mate during the latter part of the day.

"After walking effortlessly for miles together, we finally reached a beautiful palace that was glowing. My attendants took me into a hall that had a tub filled with some sparkling liquid. I was made to sit on a couch that made me feel as comfortable as a baby would feel in its mother's womb. The couch was special. I felt supremely relaxed for the first time in my life.

"One woman then started removing the clothes off my body even as another applied a sweet-smelling lotion on my shoulders and massaged them gently. I could hear a pleasant music in the background. Gradually the massage extended to the other parts of my body and with every touch I could feel my inhibitions leaving my mind. The music now turned more romantic as my masseuse reached out to various love centers of my body. I was truly in love with the beautiful women around me and my body was aching for a union with them."

She stopped narrating the dream for a moment and looked at him cutely. Her eyes were filled with the mischief that the universe could not contain. The story and her narrative left him open-mouthed and he did not even realize that she paused narrating the story. She filliped her finger against his ear and brought him back to his senses. She laughed alluringly at the little drool around the corner of his mouth.

"I got up the couch and headed to the tub. As I immersed my body in the liquid and lay in the tub quietly, my beautiful cohort unburdened themselves of their flimsy clothes and joined me in the tub. Each of them looked like a goddess of love that specialized in a unique form of love-making art. They kissed me and caressed me with a passion never seen before. The love liquid in the tub changed it sparkling colors with the increasing intensity of the activity that looked out of the world. All of us slipped into reverie and our bodies were vibrating uncontrollably.

"Almost at the pinnacle of a mind-blowing experience I looked around only to be surprised by the fact that all the beautiful women that surrounded me till then were none other than myself. I astonishingly realized that I was making love to myself. But that realization did not impede the intensity of the pleasure I was experiencing. All of us in the tub reached the climactic phase of the intensive activity almost at the same time. Precisely at the summit I could see that each one of the women simply merged with me one after the other pushing me into a spectacular series of climaxes."

She did not have to continue the story any further. He lifted her in his arms and headed straight to the bathtub whispering into her ear, "Ah! Let me see today if I can recreate the dream for you. Let it be an inhibition-free day for us." As he walked, she wrapped one hand around the back of his neck while her other hand moved downward in an attempt to keep itself busy.

Intoxicated by a story they never heard till then, the gods and goddesses of love started shooting arrows jovially at each other.

The Elevator Pitch

"Last night was a peculiarly confusing night for me," he remarked almost lamentingly. She could sense that something was bothering him. He looked a bit lost and unable to express himself. She intuitively knew that it had got something to do with the incident that happened in bed the night before. Having united after a long gap compelled by his travel abroad, the session was unfulfilling with him giving in much before than expected. She understandingly took him into her arms and pressed his head against her bosom. She asked him reassuringly, "Come on dear. Tell me what the matter is." He looked at her with almost a child-like innocence that belied the supreme authority he commanded in his social and professional circles.

Reposing a lot of faith in her ability to understand him, he started narrating the dream he saw the night before.

2

"I was standing in front of a tall building that looked like my office. From the glass windows I could see a lot of women staring at me and waving their hands. They all looked stunningly beautiful and skimpily clad. I tried diverting my attention from them but could not do so. I was feeling guilty as images of you flashed in one corner of my vision. But as the dream progressed, I was overcome by an uncontrollable urge to keep looking at the women out there."

Narrating his dream, he looked at her to see if she displayed any signs of concern or embarrassment. But she was her usual self—calm and composed as ever. Relieved that she was taking the confession in the right spirit, he continued the story.

"I walked into the building and got into an elevator. I was alone in the lift. The floor buttons got pressed by themselves and I was unsure of where I was going. As the elevator started going up I could sense some heaviness in my head. Suddenly the door opened and one of the women that I saw through the glass windows entered the elevator. She looked familiar but I could not figure out who she was. She was dressed meticulously in formal attire, but her beauty revealed itself piercingly through her dress. I could not take my eyes off her.

"As the elevator kept moving up rapidly I could feel a fatal attraction for her. She threw glances at me invitingly and I started giving in to the temptation. Even before I could make any advances she started acting strangely. She pressed herself against me and tried rousing me, but somehow I felt intimidated by her aggression. She ran her hand over my body and did all sorts of acts to entice me. Finally she had her way and I gave in amidst feelings of guilt, apprehension and an uncontrollable urge.

"Once I was in her control trying to play to her obsessive aggression she started urging me frantically to finish the act before the elevator reached its destination. I do not remember what I did but my mind was full of a pressure for an unrealistic performance. She kept urging me but I was unable to do what was needed in spite of my best efforts. The prospect of the elevator doors opening up all of a sudden exposing me to be caught in the act weighed heavily on my heart.

"Just at a time when I thought I composed myself and was in some control of the situation, something happened and the elevator started falling and moving downward at almost double the speed at which it went up. I was terrified and was feeling weightless. The strange tickling sensation between my legs was pleasurable, but it also gave me a sense of losing my own vitality. She kept exhorting me to continue the act, which I found very difficult. The elevator came to a screeching halt and I literally ran out of steam. She gave a disparaging look at my stained trousers and walked out of the elevator in a huff. Feeling drained of energy, I just collapsed in the elevator and I could feel all the women that I saw earlier laughing at me mockingly."

She listened to his dream patiently. Allowing him time to come back into reality, she hugged him, and running her fingers through his frizzy hair spoke, "Dear! Do not worry. I understand your predicament. You seem to be getting obsessed with your professional targets and deadlines. I think you are trying to accomplish too many things in too short a time. You apparently have been bitten by a bug called the elevator pitch in which you are expected to create miracles within such short a span that an elevator takes to reach its destination floor. But trust me dear, bed is not an elevator; nor do you need to be able to sell your capabilities in a ridiculously short duration. The bed for us is a vehicle of a long journey. Time never is a constraint for me or for you. I will show you the bed-pitch."

Having said that she kissed him and calmed his nerves before embarking on a beautiful ride across the love land called the bed. As they both lay on the bed after the longest ever session of love-making in their married life, she asked him with a grin, "So! How did you like the bed-pitch?" Kissing him passionately on his lips, she poked him, "I am sure I am not bad as my competitor in the elevator." He looked at her gratefully.

The gods of love chuckled at the prospect of trying the elevator pitch themselves, but not before appreciating her broadmindedness that helped her mend her partner's ways.

The Candle Dream

"Do you know what it means when a woman dreams about candles?" she asked him provocatively.

"Before your mind starts thinking of something else let me tell you the dream I saw last night," she said and continued, "I was inside a room that was cold and had a thousand candles arranged in a very visually appealing manner. I was sitting on a bed in the middle of the room. None of the candles was lit up. There was a transparent enclosure of ice around me that made me shiver with cold.

"It looked like I was waiting for someone. I was wearing a dress that was revealing but I was happy and not the least embarrassed that someone would come to see me in such a dress. There was a knock on the door and my mother walked in first. She looked at me affectionately, lighted a candle and then disappeared from there.

Next came in my father. He walked into the ice enclosure and kissed me on my forehead. He did not utter a word about my dress. He went and lighted another candle. After that, my family and friends came in one after the other and lighted one candle each. I saw in my dream many unknown faces too.

"Finally there was one candle left unlighted. With one less than a thousand candles lighted up, the ice enclosure around me started to melt but I was still feeling cold. I was still waiting for someone and was not sure who I was waiting for. The flimsy dress around my body did little to make me feel warm. Nevertheless the room now looked bright and resplendent.

"Minutes and hours passed with me sitting and watching the candles glow steadily. The unlighted candle intrigued me and I was wondering why no one came in to light it up. The candle looked special and stood out from the other candles. There was a look of majesty about that candle. I was yearning for someone to come and light it up.

"Around the time when the coldness around me was getting too uncomfortable, I heard a pleasant knock on the door and the door opened slowly. I looked at the door anticipating someone, but did not see anyone. I could sense a breeze outside my ice enclosure as the candles fluttered. The special candle started growing in size and in no time was head and shoulders above the others. The next moment the candle lighted up by itself and started glowing splendidly. The flame seemed to be touching the roof and in an attempt to reach the skies.

All other candles vanished from there as if submitting themselves to the supremacy of the mighty one.

"My heart was filled with an inexplicable joy at the sight of the candle that I was waiting to glow. The ice enclosure around me melted completely. Quite expectedly my clothes evaporated and I was now sitting stark naked on the bed, bathed in the newfound warmness. I developed a strange reverence for the candle that gave me the much needed warmth. I found myself moving effortlessly and uncontrollably towards the towering candle. With a bit of hesitation I touched it. The more I touched the candle the more I found myself obsessed with it. Every touch created ripples of sensual feelings in my heart and mind. Suddenly I found myself being stroked by an invisible hand. The hand was all over my body and I was in the midst of an experience that I cannot give words to. As I looked around, I could see each of the faces that came in and lighted up the candles. They seemed to be happy about my situation. Neither they nor I displayed any feelings of embarrassment. The invisible hand continued its work even as my well-wishers looked over and the candle spread its warmth in every corner of my body."

He listened to her story with great attention and tried to relate it to himself. He guessed that the dream had to do with her happiness about their marriage being finally accepted by her family after a lot of initial reluctance and resistance; but he did not want to analyze it any further. Lighting up a candle that was on the table, he asked her persuasively, "Now that I have lighted up the candle, is it possible that the invisible hand in your dreams was in fact mine?"

She looked at him with eyes drunk with the effects of the dream she just narrated. Gods and goddesses of love sat down for a beautiful candle light dinner.

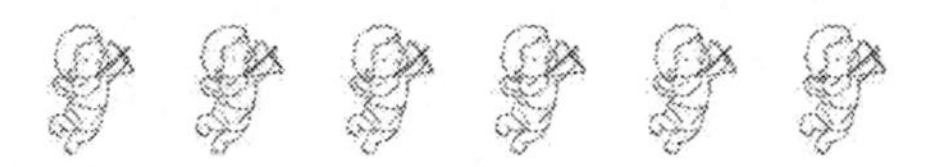

Kisses in the Tunnel

"I saw a strange dream of kisses," he said excitedly. Feigning jealousy, she asked him curiously, "So, what about the kisses?"

"I was in a train that was traveling through vast plains. The train had its roof open to the sky that met the land in all directions at a long distance. The horizon had an elusive appeal to it. My journey seemed to be towards the horizon and it was a purposeful journey. I was on my way to meet at the horizon someone very special to me.

"As the train kept racing past I was lost in contemplation. My heart was jumping with joy in anticipation of some pleasurable experience. The next moment I saw myself sitting inside the engine room of the train. The driver was a woman with beautiful lips as red as apples. She smiled at me and carried on minding her own business of driving the train. I reached out to

her and touched her luscious lips. She turned towards me and kissed me on my cheek before going back to her usual work. Reveling in the unexpected luck I ran my hand across my cheek only to realize that her kiss was indeed embossed on my cheek and I could feel the bulge vividly. I felt the experience strange.

"The train kept moving at a maddening pace. Suddenly I could see a tunnel appearing out of nowhere amidst the plains. The train slowed down as it approached the tunnel. The driver got off the engine room as the train entered the tunnel. Darkness replaced the brightness that existed till then.

"My heart that was light till then began becoming heavy as the train chugged through the dark tunnel. I started feeling apprehensive for some unexplained reason—it was not the darkness, more probably it was the loneliness. As the train passed through the tunnel I could feel a prickly sensation all over my body. The sensation was not very unpleasant, though. I was anxiously waiting for the train to come out of the tunnel, but the journey seemed to be protracted.

"The train kept moving at a snail's pace through the tunnel and through the darkness. The prickliness persisted and I did not know why it was happening. After considerable time spent in the tunnel, the train came out and again picked up its original speed. For a while I was blinded by the sudden exposure to sunlight that touched my skin warmly. As I regained my normal vision I could again see the vast plains around me. Looking back, I was surprised by the fact that the tunnel no longer existed. It vanished as if by some magician's trick. The prickly sensation on my body was gone now, but I felt something strange about myself.

"I looked at myself and was shocked momentarily that I did not have the tiniest of the threads covering my body—I was sitting in the engine room with my bare body exposed to the elements. The lady driver who got down at the entrance of the tunnel now appeared suddenly and was doing her usual business of driving the train. She looked at me lustfully and made her intentions amply clear to me by biting her lower lip with her sparkling white teeth and rolling her tongue over her lips. I stood beside her and was about to touch her when the prickly sensation appeared again. When I looked at my body I shivered at the sight of a bulge on my hand. The bulge had the shape of the driver's lips. I instinctively ran my hand over my cheek and could feel that the embossed kiss still remained.

"The very next moment I could see that the bulge replicated itself rapidly to cover almost every part of my body. I now had my entire body embossed, stamped and tattooed with kisses.

"As the train raced towards the horizon I was in a state of utter confusion—an enticing beauty inviting me to explore her and a badly out of shape body covered with kisses that were causing a mild prickly sensation. The prospect of meeting my special one at the horizon added to the confusion—I did not want to be seen with my body literally tattooed with prickly kisses. I frenetically started rubbing my saliva on to the kisses as if to get rid of them even as the driver continued her advances towards me.

"Amidst all this confusion the train again entered a tunnel and there was darkness all around. My heart now was filled with a baffling sense of dissatisfaction, the reason for which I did not know. The horizon was still far off, the driver was gone, there was darkness around and my body was covered with prickly kisses that would not go away. I woke up from my dream and saw you sleeping pleasantly beside me. The sense of relief I got when I realized that what I saw was just a dream was incredible."

She looked at him confusedly trying to analyze what the dream meant. She thought she knew some of the reasons, but stopped short of attributing every aspect of the dream to the reasons she knew. She kissed him on his cheek and playfully exclaimed, "Dear! What is this bulge on your cheek? Is it my kiss?" He laughed lightheartedly at her naughtiness. But behind the naughtiness she was creating a magnificent plot for a different kind of foreplay. As the cosmic act began he found himself doing things to her that he did not do before. At the point of union he heard her tell him breezily, "Dear. You will not see this dream anymore."

The gods and goddesses of love were wondering what she interpreted of the dream. They went to the love library and got busy reading up a book on psychology.

Naughty Quotes to Wind Up

"It is all between the legs. You don't do it with the thing in between your ears"

"Love does not make babies. It is sex that does it"

"Kids are testimonies of love and make you forget sex"

"Without good understanding between couples, 'Love and Sex' will sound like 'Lose and Vex'"

"Self-love is not bad—but better, find someone to make love to"

"Ten minutes is both long and short. It depends on whether you are stuck in traffic or if you are making love"

"Ten minutes is neither long nor short when you are stuck in traffic but still get to make love"

"The ultimate realization happens in a moment"

"It is better to be a loser in a good game of sex than to be a winner in a bad game"

"Sex according to many women is usually a one-man show. More than one man is still not a norm"

"How does it matter if love came first or sex?"

"Don't discourage kids from talking about love and sex. It is possible that they can make a lot of money writing about the subject when they grow up—just like the author of this book is doing"

"Interestingly, my wife and I got married on the same day"

"Not all four-letter words are bad—I'm talking about love"

L♥VE SPACE

Scribble y♥ur l♥ve n♥tes

ABOUT THE AUTHOR

Krishna took to writing by the encouragement of many of his family, friends and colleagues at work. He self-published his first book titled "The Rustic's Collection of Humorous Stories".

A mechanical engineer from BITS-Pilani, Krishna also holds a higher degree in management studies from SP Jain Institute of Management and Research, Mumbai. He cherishes his association with two of India's premier educational institutions and hopes to give back in good measure to his alma maters.

Krishna also has written on a variety of technical subjects like project management, quality, technology and business strategy. As an entrepreneur he experimented with business concepts that have a potential for inclusive development. He believes in challenging the status quo (as attributed to him by one of his closest friends) and keeps trying new things.

He is the happiest when at home, enjoying the company of his beautiful wife and their two young sons.

As a writer he aspires to brighten up a billion faces and lighten up a billion hearts.